# The Final Stand

**The Empty Sword Saga, Volume 3**

Jonathan Zobel

Published by Jonathan Zobel, 2024.

This is a work of fiction. Similarities to real people, places, or events are entirely coincidental.

THE FINAL STAND

**First edition. May 6, 2024.**

Copyright © 2024 Jonathan Zobel.

ISBN: 979-8224549221

Written by Jonathan Zobel.

# Table of Contents

To all my family, friends, and fans who have been cheering me on. And a huge thanks to my Editor Savannah Lewis of the Wonder Edits and my Illustrator Kelli Cork. I couldn't have made it without you!

# Pronunciation Guide.

Horiton. Hor-i-Ton
Ibexian. Eye-Bex-ian
Flitnao. Flit-Nay-Oh
Vesuvian. Ves-Sue-Vee-an
Lulandal. Loo-Lan-doll
Kittrian. KIT-tree-an
Hannela. Han-EH-la
Geltian. Gel-TEE-an
Areiop. ARE-ee-op
Annalio. ANN-al-leo
Groman. GROW-man
Blakmian. BLOKE-me-an
Trodontian. Tro-DON-tea-an
Windmere. WIND-mere
Vulant. Vu-LANT
Prariat. PRAYER-ee-at
Galent. Gay-LENT
Trakken. TRA-ken
Saralia. Sa-RAIL-lee-ah
Altimi. ALL-ti-me
Unkarian. Un-KAR-ee-an
Amronian. Am-RON-ee-an
Felinad. Fell-EE-nad

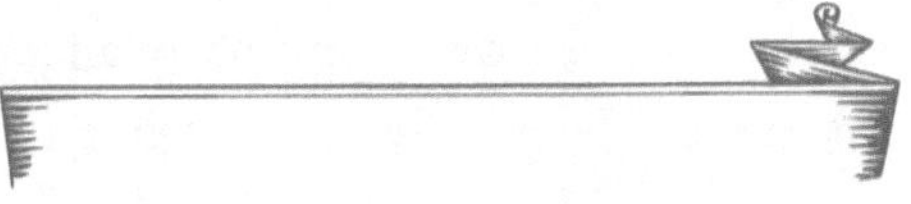

# Chapter 1. Sadness.

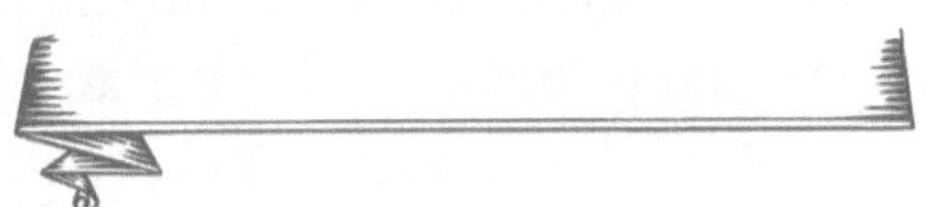

Stephen watched as the movers closed the door on the back of the truck and then turned to face him. He gave them a slow wave, and the driver returned the gesture as the other man made sure the door was secure. Then, both men got into the cab as the driver leaned his head out of the open window.

"We'll drop this off at the house in a few hours! No need to be there when we arrive!" the driver called to Stephen over his shoulder. "Take all the time you need to say goodbye!"

"Thank you!" Stephen shouted back as the truck's engine roared to life and rumbled away. Stephen then turned, went back into his old house, and saw just how empty it was, now. All the furniture was now on the truck heading to its new home; all he needed to do was get the remaining boxes and find his sister, and they could be on their way.

He slowly walked through the empty house and up a flight of stairs to where his sister's room was. Halfway up, he spotted a picture still on the wall and gently picked it up and looked at it. It was of himself, his parents, and Victoria, all at the first martial arts tournament she had won. He and his parents were standing behind Victoria, who was proudly holding her gold medal and smiling despite an impressive black eye. Stephen smiled and tucked the picture under his arm as he reached the top of the stairs before stopping when he heard Victoria softly crying to his right. He quietly entered her room and saw her looking at another photo of their family; this time, it was at a nearby state park at sunset with the setting sun behind them and an incredible view of the land below the hill they were standing on.

"Do you need a few more minutes?" Stephen asked quietly.

Victoria sniffed, folded the picture up, and placed it in her pocket before standing to face her brother. "No. I think I'm all done here," she replied softly.

"I found one you missed," Stephen said, holding out the picture he had retrieved.

Victoria took it and let out a laugh. "I remember that tournament! I still can't believe they let that kid who gave me the black eye take third place."

"Maybe it was pity for what you did to him after he gave it to you."

"I guess I did break his nose pretty badly."

The twins shared a quiet laugh before going quiet once more, as neither knew quite what to say.

After a few moments, Stephen managed to break the silence: "Are those the only boxes left?"

"Oh, uh, yes, they are," Victoria replied. "I just need to seal them up, and we can put them in the car."

"Sounds good."

Victoria quickly taped the boxes closed, and she and Stephen loaded the remaining boxes in their car and closed the trunk.

Then, they turned back to face the house, and Stephen sighed and looked at his sister. "Do you want to take one last look inside before we leave?"

"If you want to," came her quiet reply.

The twins then went back inside the house and stood in their entryway, looking at the adjoining dining room. Stephen looked back at the doorway and felt a shiver go down his spine as he remembered that day just a few weeks ago when the police chaplain arrived at their door and broke the news that their parents had been killed in a car accident. The following weeks were a blur of emotions and paperwork as they were saddled with the responsibility of taking care of the family estate. Their great aunt Belinda had done her best to help, but there was still a lot to do. Their parents had stated before that the house was theirs to do with as they pleased, but they had not written a proper will. Thus, the large earnings their father had from his partnership with a major tech company had all been lost in the legal battle that ensued with their estranged family. They won the house, but Stephen and Victoria had decided to sell it and move in with Belinda, as they couldn't stand living there due to all the emotional weight that hung over them while they were inside.

"It all happened so fast." Victoria's voice broke Stephen's train of thought. "Are you sure we made the right choice?"

"I'm not sure, but I think it's best that we should be with family right now," he replied. "Besides, I don't think we could have afforded this place on our own, especially since we both worked part-time."

"But moving a whole state away?"

"Belinda readily offered us each a room at no charge to us. All we had to do was help with the farmstead, and she said she'd try to get us better jobs in her town."

"But...."

"It's not like we had a lot keeping us here. Most of our friends moved away to attend college, and our church is closing down since our pastor left."

Victoria didn't respond; she didn't know what she could say. She knew that Stephen was eager to get away from the house he used to love so much. Her memories here did make it more painful to stay but also painful to leave. She had tried to talk to Stephen about it before, but he didn't seem to understand.

"Getting away from it all will be good for us," Stephen said, reaffirming his position.

"Maybe it will," Victoria agreed quietly.

"Come on, Tori, we've faced down monsters, evil kings, and entire armies together! We can handle this...." Stephen's voice trailed off as Victoria noticed his eyes begin to water. Stephen quickly looked away from her as he went to go back outside. Victoria followed him slowly, quietly whispering her goodbyes to the house as she closed the front door behind her. She saw Stephen had already started the car and was now waiting for her. She quickly got into the passenger seat and set her purse on the seat behind her. Just as she buckled her seat belt, she heard a beeping noise coming from her left hand.

"My watch?" she said in surprise. "But you have the only other one...."

Stephen shrugged. "Answer it."

Victoria pushed a button on her large watch and a small holographic projection of Belinda's head and upper body appeared above it.

"So that's where I left it!" Stephen laughed.

Belinda looked down in surprise and then turned to face Victoria.

"So that's how you work this confounded thing! I must say, it is very impressive. Are you on your way yet?" Belinda asked.

"Hi, Aunt Belinda! We're just leaving now; we should be there in a few hours if we stop for fuel on the way," Victoria replied.

Belinda started to reply but was cut off by Annie's voice.

"Can you ask them to get..." Annie started, but she was quickly interrupted by Belinda.

"No, I will not ask them to get you more! You've eaten through this week's supply already, and thus you will have to wait!"

"Aww," came Annie's subdued reply.

"Now, then, drive safely, you two. We'll see you in a few hours."

"See you then," Victoria replied before Belinda's image disappeared. She then turned to her brother with a sly smile. "Hey, Stephen?"

"Yeah?" Stephen replied.

"We're stopping, right?"

"Yup. I'll make sure we can grab some before we hit the road again."

"Perfect."

The twins shared a short laugh as they continued on their journey, but soon, all that was left was silence as the twins contemplated their future with their great aunt Belinda and Annie.

A few hours later, they arrived at their Aunt Belinda's farm. The movers had just finished their work and were just starting up the truck and preparing to leave. The men waved to Stephen and Victoria as they parked their car by the house and climbed out. The twins returned the wave and turned back to see their great aunt Belinda was on the porch with a gentle smile on her face.

Belinda looked up to see the moving van disappear around a corner and then looked back at Victoria. "All clear!" Belinda called out.

Victoria knew what was coming next and turned around to see her best friend Annie appear behind her. Annie was from another world she and her brother had visited several times now, and she had come with them into their world on their last visit when her brother Groman realized that it was too dangerous for her to stay. Now, the young Kittrian girl was running towards Victoria, her arms open wide, and quickly caught Victoria in a vice-like hug.

"I thought you might need a hug," Annie said quietly. Victoria was caught off-guard but quickly returned the gesture, the emotions from that morning making her eyes water again.

"Thank you, Annie," Victoria whispered.

Stephen watched the two girls hug as he opened the trunk of the car and looked at the few remaining boxes they had to carry in. He turned back to look at Annie and Victoria as they began to walk away, their arms over each other's shoulders. "Guess I should just leave them be," he said quietly to himself as he reached in for a box.

"Are these all going in?" Belinda's voice came from beside Stephen as he turned to see her short-but-muscular frame next to him.

"Yeah, this is the last of it. You don't have to help carry anything in; I can handle it," Stephen responded.

Belinda quickly picked up the largest box and winked at Stephen. "Just because I'm older than you doesn't mean I can't help."

Stephen chuckled, and the two of them quickly finished unloading the car as the girls moved over to the bench swing on Belinda's porch.

Victoria sat down on the swing and watched as the sun was just starting to set over the trees. Annie soon joined her on the swing and began to sway it back and forth slowly.

As the two of them sat on the bench, Victoria looked over at Annie. Her long white hair was nearly glowing orange in the dusky light. She wondered how long it would take to get used to seeing her in modern clothes. It was such an odd contrast to the flowing dresses and cloaks she would wear in the other world that suited her different appearance. Now, she sat next to Victoria wearing a plain red hoodie and loose-fitting jeans that were covered in grass and mud stains from helping Belinda work the farm as well as a pair of muddy rubber boots. If it weren't for her cat-like eyes, pointed ears, color-changing skin, long white hair in two braids down her back, and extra digits on her hands and feet, she might pass for a human. But even with a different look, she still seemed out of place, and Victoria knew she felt that way too.

"How are you doing, Annie? Have you gotten used to my world yet?" Victoria asked quietly.

Annie took a moment and sighed before she spoke: "I'm doing okay. Honestly, I'm not sure I will ever be fully used to it." She tugged at her hoodie before looking back to Victoria. "Your clothes are strange, a lot of your food tastes weird, and I really don't understand why so many of the people here are so preoccupied with stuff. In Lulandal, we mostly focused on survival and living a simple, peaceful life."

"Yeah, that was something I noticed in my time there. It always seemed so peaceful... except when it wasn't. I wish I could have been there without some big emergency or enemy attacking."

"Yes. I'm sure you would have loved living in Areiop with me and Groman..." Annie's voice trailed off as she looked back towards the forest.

Victoria knew what Annie was thinking about, and she tried to figure out what she could say. "You're worrying about Groman again, aren't you?"

"Yeah, these past two years have been hard, what with not hearing anything from him."

"I'm sure. I do know you have been able to find things here to keep you busy. Just like...." Victoria gave Annie a wry grin as she pulled out a big bag of gummy worms and held them out to Annie, who eagerly took the bag and began helping herself to the sugary treats.

Annie barely managed a "thank you!" in between worms as she continued gulping them down.

Victoria then turned back to the forest and sighed. "At least I know a way to help with your pain," she said quietly.

Annie set the bag down and slid closer to Victoria. "I'm sorry, Tori. I wish I could say I know how you feel. But since I was very young when my own parents died, I really don't remember much when it happened. So I can't really feel what you're going through. But if it helps, I'm here to listen if you need to talk."

The two girls sat in silence for a few minutes, their porch swing gently swaying from an autumn breeze, then Victoria spoke up: "When people say that I've lost my parents, they don't seem to realize that isn't everything I lost. We were all so close as a family, I feel like I've lost two of my best friends! Not to mention our plan for the future within Dad's company. But while we were settling the estate, it was taken over by the vice-CEO, and we were excluded from the partnership. Now...everything is gone." Victoria looked at her friend, her eyes full of tears, and Annie quickly reached out and hugged her.

"You haven't lost everything; Auntie Belinda and I are still here," Annie said softly. "And besides, aren't they in a better place with The One Above now?"

Victoria didn't respond but returned the hug from Annie.

The two girls stayed together for a few minutes until Victoria sensed someone standing behind them. She turned her head and saw Belinda standing silently by the door. She had a weak smile on her face, and her eyes were watering, too, but she quickly wiped them away with her sleeve.

"Dinner is ready whenever you two are," Belinda said quietly. "If you need more time, I'll keep it warm for you."

Belinda went back inside the house, and shortly afterwards, the girls got up from the swing and walked inside the farmhouse to join Stephen and Belinda for dinner.

Just as they were finishing the last of the food, Stephen looked out of a window that was facing the woods and spotted a column of smoke rising from the trees in the dim remains of daylight.

"Hey, look at that!" he said in a worried tone.

Belinda quickly got up from her seat, walked to the window, and looked at the smoke too.

"A campfire?" Annie asked quietly.

"Not on my property," Belinda responded coldly.

"Maybe we should check it out. It almost seems like it's in the same spot as the gateway...." Stephen's voice trailed off as he realized he probably shouldn't have said that, as Annie gasped and ran for the door, grabbing her green cloak on the way out.

"Annie! Wait!" Victoria called after her, and she hurried to the door.

Belinda and Stephen grabbed some flashlights that were hanging by the door and quickly followed the girls as they ran into the forest.

Soon, the group had found what they were looking for: a large structure made of trees and vines grown together in a sort of tube with a large hole in the side. The tube itself and the immediate area around it were singed, but the fire seemed to have burned itself out as they reached it.

"Do you think the gateway still works?" Annie asked worriedly.

Stephen carefully walked over and went through the hole inside the wall. He then came back out and looked up at the moon overhead. "I don't think I will ever get used to that," he said with a sigh of relief.

"What do you mean?" Victoria questioned.

"One moon outside; three moons inside," Stephen replied.

"So it still works. That's good," Belinda said with relief.

"What do we do, now?" Victoria asked.

"I'd say we go back home," Belinda replied. "We don't know what may have started the fire; it may have been just a small forest fire and not any reason to be concerned."

"But..." Annie interjected before Belinda cut her off again.

"Besides, even if we were needed over there, we have no way of knowing that, nor do we have our weapons. We should regroup at home and figure out what to do from there."

"That sounds like a plan to me," Stephen replied.

The group went back through the woods and to the house, where they sat around the table and discussed what had happened over glasses of tea.

"Groman told us that we needed to stay put until he told us otherwise," Stephen said firmly. "It's for Annie's protection."

"I agree that we need to honor our promise to Groman to protect Annie at all costs, but what about Lulandal itself? What if that fire was started on purpose by some enemy trying to keep us out?" Victoria countered.

"And what if Groman needs our help, but he can't contact us?" Annie added.

"You should be patient and wait for his message," Belinda replied.

"I'm tired of waiting!" Annie said while standing up from her chair. "I want to see my brother and my home again!"

"Calm down, Annalio," Belinda said firmly, "I'm sure you'll be able to return soon enough."

"How about now?" Stephen said in a perplexed tone.

"Huh?" Victoria asked.

Stephen said nothing but pointed at a nearby window.

Annie walked over to it and saw a flash of red fly through the light cast by the interior lights. She opened the window and whistled a familiar three note tune, and a blur of red flew inside, chirping like a bird.

"Is that...?" Victoria started before watching the little flying lizard dart towards Stephen and land on his head.

"Little flyer?" Stephen replied with a groan. "Yup."

Annie rushed over to Stephen and gently picked up the lizard, who began purring in her hand as she removed a piece of parchment from its tail.

"I don't believe it!" Belinda said in amazement.

"It's a message from Groman!" Annie squealed in delight. She quickly unrolled the parchment and began to read the message.

My dearest Annalio,

Not a day has gone by that I have not thought of you these two long years. I apologize for not writing to you and sending you away, but I have been very busy, and I wanted to ensure your safety. My only regret is not hugging you one more time, for I am afraid this is the last time you will hear from me.

Annie stopped reading, her eyes welling up with tears, before she dropped the parchment and fled from the room. Stephen and Victoria watched her leave before Stephen picked up the letter and continued.

The battles against Falron have been increasing in their devastation and intensity. Areiop has recently fallen, with my army now busy taking care of the refugees. Our losses continue to mount without any hope of victory in sight. Most of the soldiers have lost all morale and I with them. Windmere, Vulant, Ripper, and I have planned one last attack to try and slow Falron's advance. But I do not have high hopes for it succeeding. So I am asking you to stay with Stephen and Victoria, where you are safe. I am truly sorry it has come to this. I have failed you and our lands. Do not try to come rescue me, as you would only be walking into Falron's clutches, and I could not bear it if you were harmed again. I wish you the best in the other world. May The One Above watch over you all your days.

Your loving brother, Groman.

Stephen slowly lowered the letter, his own eyes wide with shock. He looked over at Belinda and saw she had a similar expression. Victoria had her face turned away, but he could tell she was trying to hide her own tears.

"What do we do now?" Stephen asked quietly.

"We go save my brother," came Annie's reply.

The trio looked over at the doorway and saw Annie in her green Kittrian cloak with a cold and determined look on her face.

"Annie, Groman told us to keep you here where you will be safe..." Belinda began before being cut off by Annie.

"Safe? If my brother falls, then not only will Lulandal, but this world may as well! It is only a matter of time before his forces find the gateway and then they will invade Earth! While I am not sure they would be a match for the military forces here, it would still reveal the presence of Lulandal to a world that would undoubtedly exploit it for its own greed! I cannot allow that to happen to my home! So who's with me?"

The group looked at each other in silence before Stephen spoke up: "I'm with you and Groman to the end."

"Me too," Victoria echoed.

"But I will say that we need time to prepare; we need to gather food, weapons, and other supplies before we go in," Stephen added.

Annie looked annoyed but nodded her head in agreement.

"I'll start gathering some food we can take," Victoria said as she went into the kitchen with Annie following her.

"I'll handle the weapons," Stephen said with a smile.

"Do you even know where they are?" Belinda asked as she left the room.

Stephen's eyes went wide before he turned red and looked down at his hiking boots in embarrassment. "No," he admitted ashamedly.

Belinda reappeared from the hallway with a large steamer trunk in her arms. She set it down with a thud and opened it with an old skeleton key.

Stephen hurriedly looked inside to see what they had. To his delight, he saw his one-handed sword and shield, another one-handed sword, Belinda's black and red two-handed sword, Victoria's tekkō kagi, and four daggers along with a crossbow and composite bow from their last adventure. He picked up his sword and pulled it partway out of the sheath, looking at his reflection in the spotless blade. "Hello, old friend," he mused as he strapped the sword to his waist and the shield to his back.

"I've done my best to keep them ready just in case we needed them for something," Belinda said with a grin. "Annie insisted."

"Speaking of our Kittrian guest, did she lose her dagger somewhere? I don't see it in the chest," Stephen said.

"She was with Victoria a moment ago," Belinda said.

"She's not here!" Victoria called from the kitchen.

"I'll check her room," Belinda said with a worried expression on her face.

Belinda disappeared up the stairs as Victoria entered the living room with two backpacks full of food. "This should be enough for a few days at least, and I hope Great Aunt Belinda doesn't mind my cleaning out her granola bar stash since they don't expire for a while."

"You know whatever is in the house is yours too!" Belinda called from above them. "And I don't see Annie anywhere up here!" Belinda rushed down the stairs again and grabbed her sword as well as the crossbow and a quiver of bolts from the chest. "I think she's already gone ahead of us."

"Then, we have no time to lose!" Victoria said in a panic as she grabbed her own weapons and tossed a backpack to Stephen as all three of them raced outside.

It was hard going as the trio raced through the woods in the moonlight. Branches and roots clawed at their exposed skin and tried to trip them as they pressed on at a breakneck pace. Soon, they arrived at the charred gateway and hurried inside.

"Annie!" Victoria called out, only to hear her own voice echo through the tunnel.

"Careful," Stephen warned. "If we call out too much, we may attract some attention from someone we don't want to know we're here."

"Annalio! Come back here, now!" Belinda's voice boomed through the darkness.

"Or I guess we just don't care," Stephen muttered under his breath.

"Wait! I see some light in the distance!" Victoria said excitedly.

"That may not be a good thing, but judging how the burn marks end nearby, I'd say whatever fire charred the gateway isn't still going over there," Stephen remarked.

"Then, let's go towards the light. I'm sure that's where Annie is," Belinda said.

The trio resumed their quick pace, and soon, they spotted Annie's green cloak disappear around a corner, where the light was getting much more intense.

"Annie! Wait!" Victoria shouted breathlessly.

The group rounded the corner and slid to a stop in horror at what they saw. The once-familiar wooden walls of a city and the trees covering it were ablaze with a shocking intensity, and in front of it all was a little figure in a green cloak on her knees.

"It's Areiop..." Victoria said in shock.

"I know..." Stephen replied. "And it's still burning."

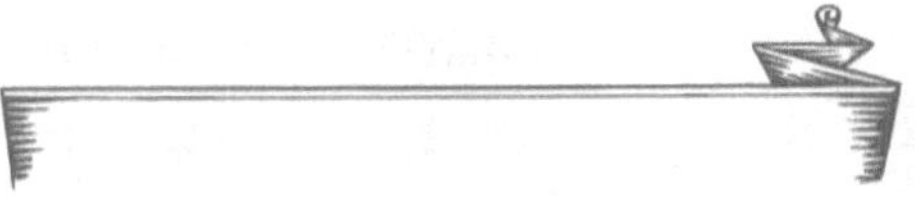

# Chapter 2. Reluctant Reinforcements.

Victoria looked up at the inferno that was busy consuming Areiop as she slowly approached Annie's still figure. Just as she reached her, Annie turned, and Victoria could plainly see the tears in her eyes reflecting the flames above them.

"This was my home..." Annie whimpered softly. "Even if it was only a few months, I felt at home here with him."

Victoria put her hand on Annie's shoulder. "I know this must hurt a lot, but we can't stay here. Whoever did this might still be nearby," she said in a soft but firm tone.

"Who...wait! There are thousands of people who live here! They must need help!" Annie said as she jumped to her feet and sprinted through the opened sally port in the main gate.

"Annie! No!" Stephen shouted but to no avail. Annie was already inside.

"We have to go after her!" Victoria replied back as she, too, ran inside.

Stephen and Belinda followed closely behind her, trying to avoid the burning debris all around them. They chased Annie to a large open area that Stephen remembered was the same square where they had their victory celebration two years ago after defeating The Shadowed One. Then, he saw Annie running from house to house, checking inside the windows and unburned doorways, looking for survivors.

"Hello! I am Annalio, Groman's sister! I and my friends are here to help!" Annie called out every few minutes. It seemed that with every call going unanswered, she was getting more desperate. She kept walking but soon fell to her hands and knees, seemingly out of breath.

"What's wrong with her?" Victoria said as the group rushed to Annie.

"The Kittrian are weak to high amounts of heat; it literally drains their energy. Annie could never really handle the summers where we live," Belinda replied. She turned to Stephen. "Stephen, we need to get her and ourselves out of this death trap."

"I know," Stephen said. He walked over to Annie, picked her up, and threw her over his shoulder as gently as he could.

"Let me go! They need help!" Annie started weakly shouting.

"Groman's letter said that they had gotten all of the refugees out of the city and to safety. There is nobody alive here but us! But we won't be if we stay any longer!" Stephen shouted back.

Annie started trying to kick him with her metal legs, but she had little strength left, and Stephen continued walking to Victoria and Belinda when he heard Annie call out again: "There's someone over there! Hey! We're over here! We're here to help you!"

Annie gave Stephen the hardest kick she could manage, which made him release his grip, and the two of them tumbled to the ground. She was up on her feet in moments, albeit unsteadily, as Victoria and Belinda ran over. Stephen slowly got to his feet and looked in the same direction as the ladies and to his surprise he saw a figure walking towards them from down a street. But he had a sick feeling in his gut that something wasn't right. He then noticed how the figure seemed to keep its head lowered so that he couldn't see its face. It was only when he saw it walk through a tongue of flame that he knew what it was.

"Guys, we need to leave right now!" His voice was far more panicked than he preferred, but it did get their attention.

"What do you mean?! There's someone right there!" Annie said again, pointing at the figure.

"That's no Kittrian," Stephen answered quickly.

It was then that the figure looked up at the group, and they saw its eyes glowing purple. All four of their faces went white as the figure unhinged its jaw and let out a spine-chilling scream that echoed all around them.

"Run, Annie! Now!" Stephen shouted, drawing his weapons, as the other ladies followed suit.

Annie turned to run back the way they came, only to see, to her horror, more of the shadowy figures emerging from all sides and surrounding the group.

"What are they, Stephen?" Belinda asked in a worried tone.

"Shadow warriors...created by Falron's power. They are easily beaten with a single hit, but he can summon so many of them, it's easy to get overwhelmed."

"One hit, eh?" Belinda replied as she raised her black and red blade. "This shouldn't be too bad, then."

Suddenly, a nearby house was smashed as a huge Unkarian leapt through it like it was carboard. It looked at the small group with malice in its purple eyes.

"There's an Unkarian too!" Victoria shouted in a panic.

"Leave that monster to me!" Belinda replied. "I've felled bigger."

"Alright, here's the plan!" Stephen shouted. "When they attack, we need to focus on defending ourselves and reducing their numbers as quick as we can. Once there are few enough, I will try to clear a path for us to escape. For right now, we need to get into a circle with our backs to each other for better defense."

The group quickly got into formation with their weapons ready.

"Annie, send little flyer for help!" Victoria called out.

"Good idea!" Annie replied. She quickly pulled the lizard out of the sleeve of her cloak and looked it in the eyes. "Go get help," she told it firmly before tossing it into the air. The little lizard spread its wings and darted into the sky. Annie then rolled up the sleeves on her cloak to reveal a number of small metal spikes contained in sheathes on her forearms. She caught Victoria staring at them in surprise. "Throwing spikes," she explained. "I had to come up with something to pass the time on the farm."

Victoria nodded in approval before looking at Stephen, who was busy watching the horde slowly close in.

"I just hope we can last long enough for it to bring help," Stephen said under his breath.

Just then, one of the shadow warriors let out another shriek and all of the other shadows attacked at once. The group was doing their best to fight them off, but with every shadow felled, it seemed like two more would take its place.

"They just keep coming!" Victoria called out as she sliced two into dust with her claws.

"Look out!" Annie screamed.

The group looked up to see the Unkarian throwing a flaming wagon at them. The group scattered to avoid getting crushed.

Victoria found herself lying on the ground, looking up at the Unkarian, which had a cruel smile on its face. Just then, she heard a shriek from Belinda as she ran at the monster at full speed. The monster clasped its hands together and brought them down in an attempt to crush Belinda, but she was too quick, and she slid between its legs. Once she was behind it, she swung her sword behind her and cut the back of both of the Unkarian's legs, causing it to fall to its knees. Wasting no time, Belinda jumped up and spun her sword in a large arc, beheading the monster in midair. She landed on her feet and looked back at the Unkarian, who was already on its way to falling on its face.

She then noticed Stephen and Victoria staring at her with complete shock on their faces. "Told you I've fought bigger." She smirked.

Victoria was about to comment when she spotted three more shadow warriors appear on a nearby housetop. To her surprise, they weren't the normal Kittrian soldiers but the cat-like Amronians.

"Belinda! Above you!" Victoria screamed.

Belinda spun around just in time to see the three shadows leap down and run at her. She saw one get picked off by a spike thrown by Annie, and she swung her sword at the other two once they were close. Her sword dispatched one of them, but the other was too fast and slashed at her stomach. Belinda let out a gasp of pain before spinning around to kill the third shadow. "Those things are quick!" Belinda gasped.

"Are you okay?" Victoria asked.

"It's just a scratch, Tori. I'll be fine." Belinda answered as she clutched her chest with her right hand and holding the sword with her left.

Victoria knew she was lying; the amount of blood was evident of that. She looked for Stephen and saw him bashing another shadow with his shield. "Stephen! Belinda's hurt bad; it's now or never!" she called out.

Stephen didn't say a word but started charging towards the street they came from, holding his shield in front of him like a plow and knocking dozens of shadow warriors aside.

Belinda, Annie, and Victoria had regrouped and were now starting to follow the path Stephen was making, with Victoria keeping the shadows off their backs and Annie, weak as she was, trying to help Belinda walk.

Before they could make it, another Unkarian burst out of the house closest to Stephen and backhanded him into the square. He landed near the ladies out cold.

Belinda pushed Annie away and put both hands on her sword only to pass out from blood loss and fall as well.

Victoria looked behind her just as Belinda fell only to get blindsided by a shadow warrior's punch, sending her to the ground. Her vision began to fade as she could hear Annie's voice echoing in her mind.

"Tori!" Annie was screaming as she was valiantly trying to fight with her dagger and what few throwing spikes she had left. "Get up, Tori!" Annie threw her last spike, and it hit the Unkarian in the chest. The beast roared and threw some debris at her. She ducked, but it clipped the top of her head, sending her to the ground. "Help me, Tori!" Annie called out as she fell.

Victoria saw red, and when she came to, she noticed over a dozen shadows fading away at once. She looked down and saw her claws were dripping with blood. She saw some bodies on the ground and realized to her horror some of them were possessed kittrian soldiers. Then, she felt the ground shake as the Unkarian charged at her, only to be felled by two daggers thrown into its eyes and a third into the back of its head.

Before the monster hit the ground, the cat-like figures of Ripper and his eldest daughter Hannela leapt from the rooftops and landed near where Victoria stood.

"It's about time you showed up!" Victoria shouted at them.

"You are fortunate we were on patrol nearby!" Ripper called back.

"How many of those things are there?!" Hannela shouted.

"Too many," Ripper answered. "We have help arriving in mere moments; we need only to keep them at bay."

Just then, Victoria heard the thunder of hooves as Windmere, her son Trakken, and another Trodontian warrior burst into the square.

"Take those three with you to the healing tent!" Ripper ordered.

The trio said nothing but scooped up Annie, Belinda, and Stephen and rushed away. The three remaining warriors kept fighting, but they were being backed against a wall.

"I don't suppose you had a plan to get us out too?" Victoria muttered.

Just then, a loud shriek was heard overhead as the trio were quickly picked up by the bird-like talons of Vulant, Peregrine, and Shriken.

"As a matter of fact, I did have a plan," Ripper purred smugly.

"Well done, Daddy!" Hannela called out as she nimbly flipped up onto Shriken's back.

"Indeed, it was a good plan," Peregrine added.

"Well, we had mere moments after that Flizard appeared above our party to make one, so it had better work," Ripper said.

"Well thank you so much for the rescue! I'm glad to see you all!" Victoria shouted to her friends.

"No, thank *you* for coming back," Ripper said under his breath.

"What was that?" Victoria asked.

"He said it is good to see you too," Hannela replied.

Victoria said nothing but looked ahead to see a large encampment coming into view below them.

"That is the biggest army encampment I've ever seen!" she commented.

"It would be if it was all solders," Peregrine replied coldly.

"The Areiop refugees?"

"Yes. We were able to evacuate everybody just as the city began to burn yesterday," Vulant replied as he began to descend.

"Your brother and friends will be in the healing tent. I have to give my report to Groman," Ripper said as he walked away into the maze of tents.

"Thanks again, Ripper!" Victoria called after him. She looked around the camp and saw many people of different races wandering about, few of whom did not sport any bandaged wounds or visible injuries. There were many soldiers, too, but they all had dark bags under their eyes and empty stares as if they had seen years of relentless combat.

Victoria quickly hurried over to the tent that Ripper had directed her to, and just as she approached, she heard a familiar voice from inside.

"Watch where you are falling, Tiny!" Saralia's voice called out, followed by a loud thud and then snores.

Victoria opened the flap and saw Stephen, Belinda, and Annie all lying on cots with healers attending to their wounds. Belinda looked the worst, but Victoria knew from the sleeping form of Tiny, the Unkarian healer in front of her, that the bloodstains were just that, and Belinda's wounds were healed.

Saralia's large, half-equine form trotted over to Victoria as soon as she saw her. "Are you injured as well?" she asked as she came over.

Victoria said nothing but ran over to her and hugged her, and Saralia returned the gesture.

"Just a few bumps and bruises; nothing more," she replied. "How is my aunt?"

"Thanks to Tiny, she will be fine. He got to her just in time. She may be tough, but it will take a day or two for her to fully recover."

"I'm fine, too, thanks for asking," Stephen said groggily from his cot.

"That's a surprise. That Unkarian sent you flying nearly ten feet away with one slap," Victoria said.

"I want a rematch," Stephen said as he slowly got up from his bed.

Saralia quickly trotted over to him and helped him to his feet.

"You need to take it slow, Stephen," she said firmly.

"I'll take it slow after we beat Falron," he replied.

Just then, Groman's voice from outside interrupted their conversation.

"What do you mean she is here? I thought I made sure she was going to be kept safe!"

Groman then burst into the tent, and he looked around at the group. "What did I say about staying put until I sent for you?" he said in a low tone.

"We weren't going to let you go on a suicide mission, Groman. Like it or not, we are here to help," Victoria said firmly.

Groman sighed and looked at the twins. "Since you are here, I guess we should plan a new strategy. Meet me at my tent when you are able." Groman then turned around and left the tent.

Stephen and Victoria were surprised at their friend's behavior, and Annie was nearly at the verge of tears.

"You'd almost think he was happy to see us," Stephen quipped.

"What happened to my brother?" Annie whimpered.

Saralia walked over to Annie and put her arms around her in an embrace. "He is happy to see you, Annie. He has just been through a lot recently. Some of us thought he had given up hope these last few days, but now that you have returned, I think I caught a glimmer of it in his eye."

"Nah, that was from seeing Victoria again." Stephen chuckled.

Victoria felt her face turn red before she elbowed Stephen in the stomach, making him bend over in pain. "We should go over to his tent. Annie, please stay here with Aunt Belinda. We'll be back soon," Victoria said after regaining her composure.

Annie silently nodded as Victoria walked out. Stephen followed close behind her, still gasping for breath.

The twins quickly found Groman's tent and ducked inside. There, they found him standing over a large map of Lulandal with several daggers stuck into various cities.

"Groman?" Victoria asked quietly.

"Come in," Groman responded. He looked up at the twins as they entered, and they got a good look at him for the first time.

Victoria felt her heart break as she saw what had become of him: His once bright eyes seemed dim and sunken in, his once orderly white hair seemed grayer and rougher; he now had a rough beard that it seemed like he had never trimmed it. His once brightly polished armor was dirty and dented, and the great Empty Sword, which lay on a table nearby, was nicked and smudged.

Groman caught their stares and gave a slight laugh. "Not much left of the naïve man you once knew now, is there?"

"No, he's still standing right in front of us; he's just been through a lot and needs help even though he won't admit it," Stephen said in a gentle tone.

Groman sighed again and a weak smile crept across his face. "I will not deny: It is good to see you all again. I have lost so much over these last two years—so many soldiers, people, and places—I am glad to regain some allies."

"Two years?" Stephen asked.

"Yes," Groman replied.

"That is how long it's been for us too," Victoria commented.

"Maybe having Annie in our world linked the times in both worlds?" Stephen mused as he turned to look at the map.

Victoria looked at Groman's weary face and tried to think of something to say. "Is Falron really that big of a threat?" she asked quietly.

"Yes. He has taken several cities such as Altimi, Felinad, Cearit, The Black Peak prison, and, just recently, Areiop," Groman replied.

"Have you figured out why he is taking those particular cities?" Stephen asked.

"We are not sure, other than a few theories, anyways. We only know he is making a push towards these forests, and we are assuming he is either just making his way west or...."

"...the gateway to our world," Victoria finished.

"Yes."

"That's why you tried to burn it down," Stephen said quietly.

"What?!" Victoria gasped. "How could you say that, Stephen? We all know he wanted to see Annie again and bring her home. Groman wouldn't—"

"The fire of Areiop and the one in the gateway were separated by untouched ground," Stephen interrupted, "and he said himself that he made sure that Annie would be safe."

Groman's face fell as a tear dropped from his right eye. "It was the hardest thing I have ever done; I realize now that I was making a rash choice in blocking off my best friends from coming to my aid. I only pray to The One Above that you can forgive my actions."

"We already have, Groman," Victoria said, rushing forwards and giving him a hug.

"I might have done the same thing if I were in your place," Stephen added.

"Thank you, my friends," Groman said quietly. "I can only hope that your return means that there is indeed hope for our world to survive yet."

"That is why we are here, isn't it?" Stephen asked. "Now, what sort of strategy have you been thinking about?"

"Well, we have been trying to figure out why Falron has been taking specific cities, and our best theory is—"

Groman was interrupted by a tiny figure flying in through the door.

"Groman! The enemy was sighted turning north towards the mountains! Shall we pursue?!" the little figure shouted.

"Monaria?!" Victoria asked in surprise.

The little figure spun around and faced her, and Victoria could see it was, indeed, the little Flitnao friend she had made on her last adventure there. Her armor was nearly as worn out as Groman's, but her tired expression gave way to happiness when she saw the twins. "You have returned! Oh, thank The One Above! This must be a sign of good things to come, it..." Monaria stopped in mid-sentence as her eyes rolled back and she dropped from the air.

Victoria dove for her and managed to catch her tiny body before she hit the ground. Monaria was silent for only a moment, and Victoria knew that she was having one of her visions.

"Two shall stand, one shall fall, two shall stand, one shall fall," Monaria muttered before passing out.

Everyone else looked at each other in surprise.

"What was that?!" Stephen asked, shocked.

"I hope that wasn't one of her visions," Victoria replied.

"If it was, it might mean that one of us..." Groman began.

"Is going to die," Monaria said in her trance-like state, staring deep into Victoria's eyes.

# Chapter 3. Preparation and Planning.

Stephen, Victoria, and Groman all stared at each other in shock from what they just heard.

Stephen felt his mind racing as to what his friend had said moments ago. She may have been in a trance, but he knew her ability to know the future was genuine; she just hadn't had a lot of time to really hone it in. That didn't mean any of them were going to die, right? While he felt he was ready to give his life for his friends and sister, he could not bear the thought of watching Victoria be hurt again, let alone die. He looked at Groman and could see his face was the same tired and pained expression as it was when they saw him in the medical tent.

"This is why I told you to stay there!" Groman said angrily.

Monaria began to stir in Victoria's cupped hands.

"Groman, just because she said..." Victoria started.

"She just told you that one of us is going to die!" Groman shouted at her. He slammed his hands on the map table in frustration. "She has never been wrong before, and now, because you refused to listen to me, one of us is not going to be alive to see who will win this war!"

"Groman, listen to me," Stephen started.

"I have listened enough! Leave my tent, now! I need time to process what we were told," Groman snapped back.

Stephen and Victoria slowly walked out of the tent, but before they were outside, Groman spoke up again.

"Please refrain from telling anyone else what we heard here; I do not want my sister to know I am going to die."

The twins nodded as they left the war tent to go back towards the healing tent. By this time, Monaria was just coming to in Victoria's hands.

"What just happened?" she muttered, barely audible.

"You had another vision and blacked out," Victoria said quietly.

"I could gather that much," Monaria replied. "But what did I say?"

The twins looked at each other, wondering what to tell her.

"It was something bad, was it not? I can tell by your faces the news was very disconcerting."

Victoria held Monaria up closer to her face and whispered, "You said that two shall stand and one shall fall; you also said that one of us was going to die."

At this, Monaria gasped and was about to say something before Victoria put a finger to her lips. "You cannot tell anyone else of this. I'm afraid that this news would undoubtedly cause morale to fall to a new level and cause panic among the troops."

The tiny warrior quietly nodded before flapping her dragonfly-like wings and taking flight. "Your secret is safe with me, my friends. What are we going to do now?"

"Well, we are going to check on our friends and family who came here with us before we return to Groman and try to work out a plan. Looming death or no, we still have a world to save," Stephen said quietly.

"That seems the wisest course of action. Might I accompany you? I should like to meet this family who came here with you."

"Of course. Aunt Belinda has never met any Flitnao before, so I think she would enjoy the chance to see you," Victoria answered.

"If I may—if I am the first Flitnao she shall see—I would like to make myself more presentable. Groman asked me if I may be an ambassador to Lulandal if we were to be victorious, so I would like some practice making first contact. I shall rejoin you shortly," Monaria said before zipping away.

"I wish I could move that fast," Victoria mused.

"Come on. I'm sure Belinda has many questions for us by now," Stephen said.

When the twins arrived at the healing tent, they found Saralia, who was just exiting it.

"Is our aunt alright?" Victoria asked.

"She is awake and well, though I wish you humans would stop staring so much; it is rather embarrassing," Saralia remarked.

"She's not used to seeing someone like you, Sara," Victoria responded. "Give her time."

Saralia managed a weak smile before trotting off.

The twins entered the tent and were relieved to see Belinda on her feet, walking around.

"Oh, there you are!" she said in a worried tone. "Annie and Saralia said you had left to go see Groman?"

"That's right," Stephen answered.

"So what's the plan, then?"

"We don't know; we were interrupted by more pressing matters. We'll be meeting again tomorrow morning at sunrise."

"So we just wait until he calls us?"

The twins looked at each other with uncertainty, but before they could respond, a tiny figure flew into the room; Monaria had arrived. She was wearing a long dress made from blue and purple flower petals, and her long white hair was in a single braid down her back.

"Hello, all! Ah! You must be the family the twins spoke of! My name is Monaria, and I am an ambassador of the Flitnao people to Lulandal." She held out her tiny hand to Belinda to shake, and Belinda gingerly took it between her fingers and shook it.

"I'm Stephen and Victoria's Great Aunt Belinda," Belinda replied.

"It is a pleasure to make your acquaintance," Monaria said with a smile. She then flew back towards Victoria, landed on her shoulder, and whispered into her ear: "How did I do?"

"You were perfect," Victoria whispered back quietly.

"Thank you," Monaria replied quietly. "I want to make sure I do it right!"

"So what do you two plan to do?" Belinda asked.

"I want to talk to Groman and get some more intel before making any strategies," Stephen said.

"Something happened between you three, didn't it?" Belinda asked.

The twins looked at each other and Monaria before Victoria responded.

"Groman isn't the same man we knew two years ago. Two years of combat and losses have changed him. He's...." Her voice trailed off as she sensed a tear in her eye.

"He is losing hope nearly as fast as we have lost cities to Falron," Monaria chimed in. "Right now, even he is uncertain of what he must do."

"So this Falron is really powerful, then? Steve, you said he could control those creatures back there and create those shadows?" Belinda asked.

"Yes, those are two of his abilities," Steven replied.

"Just those two?"

"He has pyrokinesis as well."

"How did he get those powers?"

"We're not sure," Annie replied.

"Wait!" Victoria said quickly. "Remember the Sword of Embers?"

"The Sword of Embers?" Belinda asked in disbelief.

"Oh, yeah!" Stephen replied. "When he picked it up, it seemed like he just drained that blade of life. It just turned dull and grey before dissolving into dust."

"If you think he can drain the ancient weapons of their energy, that sword's power will be a major problem," Belinda said worriedly. "I should know."

"Did we tell you about that sword?" Victoria asked.

"You mentioned it, but I happen to have some experience with that blade myself. It's not one of my prouder moments. I only had it because Geltian had offered it to me, and I didn't realize he had stolen it from its rightful owners."

"Geltian stole it?!" Annie asked in surprise. "How?!"

"Those Ibexians were rather dim-witted," Victoria replied.

"I still find it hard to believe you were able to wield it," Stephen added.

"It's a long story that I may tell you later. For now, we must focus on the task at hand. I would suggest you go talk to Groman again and see if you can figure out a game plan for the coming battles," Belinda said.

"What about you?" Monaria asked.

"I have something at home that may prove useful. However, I will need some help as—Saralia, was it? —said it may take some time for my wound to fully heal. I don't want to risk reopening it by going alone," Belinda replied.

"I will be happy to send some of my Flitnao fighters to assist you," Monaria said.

"Thank you, Monaria," Belinda said with a smile.

"We'll go find Groman, then," Victoria said.

"Be careful out there," Stephen added.

Annie ran to Belinda and gave her a hug. "Please be careful, Auntie."

"I will, my dear," Belinda said, returning the hug.

The twins and Annie then left the tent and made their way back to where they had last seen Groman. As they walked, Annie broke the silence with a question.

"What is going on with my brother?" she asked.

The twins looked at each other before Stephen spoke.

"He has been worn down by two years of war and has lost most of the battles he has fought. His spirit is at its lowest point right now. If we had not come, I'm not sure what he may have done."

"But we're here now, surely that would help, right?" Annie asked earnestly.

"I think it has...well... I hope it has," Victoria answered.

"So what are we going to do?" Annie asked.

"I have an idea, but it's a stretch," Stephen responded. "I'll explain more when we get to Groman."

The trio arrived at the pavilion, where they could hear Groman talking with some of the other leaders. They paused at the door, listening to the conversation.

"Groman! We need to come up with a battle plan to deal with this threat once and for all! We cannot lose another capitol city to Falron's forces!"

The twins recognized the voice to belong to Chieftain Galent of the Trodontian tribe.

"I am aware of the situation, Chieftain Galent," Groman responded. "However, I am at a loss as to how to properly counter Falron's constant advances. With every city he takes, his numbers grow, as more people fall under his control. Our soldiers are too often afraid to go into battle against his mind-controlled forces for fear of hurting their friends and allies. Until we figure out a way to free our comrades from his control, a full assault is unlikely to happen."

"A good knock on the head worked for Victoria," Stephen said as he pushed his way into the tent. Victoria and Annie followed behind them.

Victoria noted that along with Groman and Galent, she also saw Elder Gilder of Areiop, Captain Urano of the Flitnao fighters, Windmere, King Vulant and Peregrine of Altimi, Ripper, Vesuvian of the Fire Giants, and Frostous of the Ice Dwarves all standing around a large map table.

"Please excuse the interruption," Annie said. "But we are here to help."

Groman gave the twins a cold look but said nothing, while the other leaders nodded their approval, some of their expressions changing from despair and worry to hope as they saw their heroes had returned once more.

"I have an idea for how we could regain some control of the battlefield," Stephen said as he stepped forward into the group. "During our last time here, Victoria, Annie, and myself all encountered Falron. We witnessed some of his abilities in action as well as how he may have obtained them. We saw him pick up the Sword of Embers and watched as he drained the power from it and how he could use that power as his own afterwards. We also witnessed him use his mind control abilities on our group, including on Victoria, who stands before you. It took a hard hit to her head, but we were able to bring her back to our side. What I propose to you now is that we attempt to track down any more of the ancient artifacts that have special abilities and safeguard them from Falron. Perhaps their chosen wielders are among our armies or the civilians you have helped rescue. Even if they aren't, having the artifacts in our possession might serve as a way to draw Falron out and bring him to us where we could potentially subdue him and defeat him."

The leaders looked at each other and discussed that Stephen had said.

Groman walked over to where the twins and Annie were standing. "I told you to wait until I sent for you," Groman said in a low tone.

"This threat is too big to wait around. We need to act as soon as we can," Stephen said quietly.

"Your idea has merit, Stephen," Elder Gilder spoke up from across the room, "albeit we are unsure if there are any other artifacts around or even where they are located."

"Then, begin talking with all the refugees and the soldiers. The Broken Gauntlets were known to Ripper and his family. Maybe someone will be willing to tell us where another may be found," Stephen replied.

The leaders quickly nodded and left the pavilion, leaving Stephen, Victoria, Annie, and Groman.

"Groman, what is going on?" Annie asked angrily. "Why must you be so cold to our friends?"

"Because I did not want any of you to be endangered by Falron!" Groman snapped back.

Annie put her hands over her mouth and her eyes went wide with shock at her brother's reaction. She was not used to seeing him like that.

Groman's expression fell as he sighed and turned away from them. "You have not been here to see what I have seen. So many lives lost...cities burned... friends turned into enemies. I could not live with myself if you had been given the same fate. That is why I sent you away, to keep you safe, and yet despite my best efforts, you have come here anyways and put yourself into harm's way when we have no hope of winning," he said in a defeated tone.

Annie initially said nothing but soundlessly walked over to her brother and put her hand on his shoulder. "There is always hope, dear brother. Now that we're here, we can see about bringing it back to you," she said quietly.

Groman quickly pulled her into an embrace, tears beginning to well up in his eyes. "I have missed you so much, Annalio," he said on the verge of crying.

"I've missed you, too, Groman," Annie replied.

The twins silently watched the reunion for a few seconds, not wanting to interrupt the moment.

But a Flitnao messenger burst into the tent. "General! Elder Gilder sent me to find you! They have a report of a possible artifact near Jeatut!"

"Where?" Groman asked quickly.

The messenger flew over to the map and pointed to a spot to the southwest of Jeatut. "A young Kittrian soldier revealed that his family had been caretakers of an artifact known as 'The Wanderer's Staff', and he is one of the only people who knows where it is; however, he is unsure if he is the one to wield it," the messenger replied.

"That's alright. All we need to do is keep Falron from getting his mitts on it," Stephen said. "Is he willing to take us there?"

"Certainly," the messenger replied. "He agreed to take a small group there tomorrow."

"Excellent," Victoria responded. "Please let him know that we will go retrieve the artifact with his help."

The messenger nodded and flew out of the tent.

"Well, that's some good news, already," Stephen said as he looked back at the map table. "The quicker we can get our hands on it, the better."

"But if we cannot use it, much less touch it, how are we to transport it?" Groman asked.

"Maybe we can wear thick gloves or somehow push it into a box?" Annie suggested.

"That might work," Stephen said.

Just then, the group heard the sound of some large things landing outside.

"Who goes there?!" Groman called out.

"It is I, Screnlon, and some of my personal guards. May we come inside? I have some information you may want to hear," a raspy voice responded.

"You may enter, friend!" Groman called back. He then turned to Stephen, Victoria, and Annie. "He is an elder of the Horiton and their chief archivist. If there is an artifact to be found within their territory, he would know where it is."

As Groman finished speaking, three Horiton entered the tent. There were two guards in light armor with swords on their belts on either side of the one who had spoken. The one in the middle looked rather old and walked with an ornate cane, his wings were a mottled brown and grey, and, while his face was full of wrinkles, his large yellow eyes were as bright as evening sun and seemed to sparkle when he saw the humans and Annie.

"Ah! So you must be the other chosen ones who have come to help us in our time of need!" the elder Horiton said with a smile. He held out his taloned hand for Stephen to shake, which Stephen did.

"Yes, sir. We heard that you needed help, and we are here to assist you in bringing down Falron once and for all," Stephen said.

"Very good," Screnlon replied. "Now, it has come to my attention that you are looking for artifacts of great power in order to keep them out of our enemy's hands. Is that not true?"

"That's our idea, anyways," Victoria responded.

"Well, there is one rumored to be to our north tucked deep into the mountains of the Northern Range within a shrine dedicated to a past hero of ours who was able to rally our entire nation against a threat. Nobody knows exactly where it is, what it is, or even if it still exists," Screnlon added.

"Well, if there is a chance of its existing, we need to get our hands on it before Falron does. The power to unite an entire tribe is something he would certainly want for his own," Groman replied.

"My guards here say they have an idea of its location, and they are willing to fly you there tomorrow," Screnlon said.

"Excellent. We will be ready to go by then," Stephen replied.

"Thank you, Screnlon," Groman said.

Screnlon and his guards bowed quickly and left.

Groman turned to face his friends and sister. "We have two possible artifacts to obtain. What is our plan, now?" he asked.

"Divide and conquer," Stephen replied. "We split up into two groups and each do our best to retrieve one of the artifacts."

"I shall go with the Horiton," Groman said.

"I'll go with you, brother!" Annie added quickly.

"I'll go to the artifact in the south. Maybe Windmere, Saralia, and Trakken will be willing to take us. That'll cut the travel time down significantly," Stephen said. "What about you, Victoria?"

Victoria looked at her brother and then at Groman and turned a slight shade of red. "If it's ok with you... I think I'll go with Groman and Annie."

Stephen smirked slightly but nodded his approval. "Then, you'll want to ask some other Horiton or Blackmians to go with you, so everyone has a ride," he replied.

"King Vulant and his queen may be willing to accompany us," Groman offered.

"His queen?" Annie said, surprised.

"Yes, he and Peregrine said their vows only a few weeks ago. It was a bright moment in a dark time; we had just lost Altimi, and Vulant thought that their union may help with morale," Groman responded.

"I'm very happy for them," Victoria replied.

"Now, back on topic: I've got a gut feeling that with this shrine, you may have booby traps or some unknown challenges within. You may want to see if Ripper or Hannela will go with you. I'd imagine they are experts with that sort of thing," Stephen added.

"Ripper is currently in charge of the guards around the camp. It would have to be Hannela," Groman said.

"Who else will go with you, Stephen?" Annie asked.

"I'd assume the Kittrian guard who knows where to locate the artifact at least. With Windmere and her family with us, I don't think we'd be lacking in the combat department if something were to happen," Stephen answered.

"What if something does happen?" Annie asked.

"Good question," Stephen replied.

"Wait! Our watches!" Victoria replied.

"Your what?" Groman asked.

Stephen grinned before darting out of the tent. In a few moments, a loud beeping emanated from Victoria's watch. She pressed a button, and the holographic image of Stephen appeared waving at them.

Groman jumped back in surprise. "What kind of sorcery is that?!" he nearly shouted.

"Not sorcery; technology," Stephen's hologram answered. "Our father designed this to be a handy form of two-way communication. They have an incredible range and battery life, so they would work even in this world."

"Is there anything else they can do?" Groman asked, his face dumbfounded.

"There is a taser function built in for defense, but it kills the battery after one use; it's still just a prototype," Victoria answered.

Stephen's holographic form disappeared, and the real Stephen soon rejoined his friends in the tent.

"Are there any other questions or objections to tomorrow's plans?" Stephen asked.

"I think we are all set to go," Annie replied.

Groman and Victoria nodded in agreement.

"It's settled, then. Let's get some sleep and be ready for the journey tomorrow," Stephen said.

The group all left the tents and soon found themselves in hammocks trying to sleep. Stephen had already found his Trodontian friends, and they had agreed to go with him and the Kittrian guard to locate the artifact. Vulant and Peregrine had also agreed to go with Groman, Annie, and Victoria.

Despite the good news and seemingly easy mission ahead, Stephen was restless, tossing and turning in his hammock. He couldn't get Monaria's words out of his head.

*One of us is going to die,* he thought. *What if it's Victoria?*

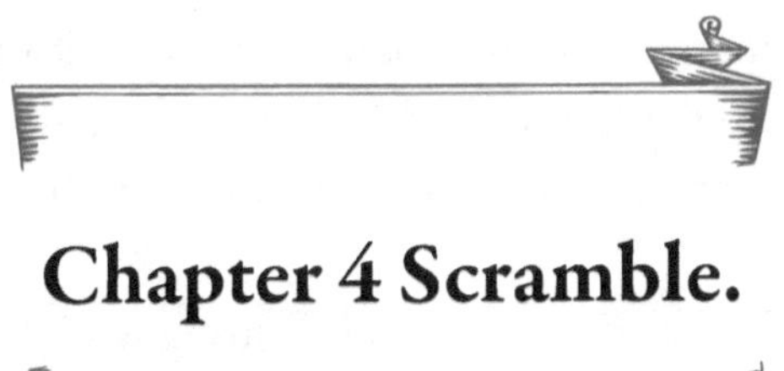

# Chapter 4 Scramble.

Victoria lay in her hammock, trying to sleep. She hadn't gotten much rest due to her mind wandering that night. She could still hear Monaria's voice in her head with her dreadful prophecy. She couldn't help but wonder what she had meant, or, worse, who was going to die.

But then something light and fluffy brushing against her face broke her train of thought. She clenched her eyes shut and tried to swat it away, but it kept coming back. She groaned and covered her face with the blanket.

"Five more minutes?" she pleaded.

"The sun is already up. I can smell someone making breakfast. We must go," Hannela's voice purred from above her.

"Why did I get stuck with you as a bunkmate?" Victoria groaned.

Hannela chuckled. "Because the one below mine was the only one available in this tent." She deftly sprang from her hammock and landed without a sound on her padded paws right next to Victoria. "Now, come along. There is no time to waste." She smacked Victoria's face with her tail one more time before sprinting for the exit.

Victoria groaned again but got up out of her hammock and looked over where she had left her claws on a small table. She picked them up and thought she felt a small jolt of energy enter her arms and flow through her body. She let out a gasp and dropped them in surprise.

"What was that? Victoria, are you alright?" Saralia's voice called out from outside the tent.

"E...everything's fine!" Victoria replied nervously.

The tent flap opened, and Saralia came halfway through, her scimitars at her tan flanks polished and ready for action.

"Cut yourself on your weapons, did you?" Saralia asked in a joking tone.

"No! N...no," Victoria stammered. "I just got a jolt from the metal, that's all."

Saralia looked at her with a raised eyebrow but said nothing as she backed out of the tent.

Victoria watched as her large, half-equine shadow walked past the tent and away from her. She took a deep breath and reached out for her claws again. This time, she felt nothing when she picked them up. Breathing a sigh of relief, she put them into their holsters at her sides and then left the tent.

She came upon the two groups who were setting out for the artifacts all around a large table with what looked like biscuits and gravy on wooden plates for each of them. Vulant and Peregrine were sitting side by side and talking to each other. Stephen was talking with Windmere and Trakken in between mouthfuls of food. The Horiton warriors, dressed in light leather armor and dark blue tunics and breeches had already finished and were watching the others with their large eyes. Saralia was busy pouring more gravy on her breakfast, her long tail swishing excitedly. Groman was standing in the shadows cast by one of the tents, his blade leaning against a large tree.

Hannela was eating some fruit that looked like a blue apple; she looked up as Victoria approached. "There is plenty of food for you, help yourself," she purred.

"You don't want any?" Victoria asked.

"Father says to avoid meat before missions; it gives the body...adverse reactions that can give your position away when stealth and silence are your only allies," Hannela said, sounding embarrassed.

"If you say so," Victoria said. She walked over to where the kettle was sitting over a fire. She noticed Annie stirring the pot while humming an unusual tune.

"What's that tune, Annie?" Victoria asked.

"Oh, it's something that I've had in the back of my mind ever since I can remember. I think I can recall Mother singing it to me when I was a baby," Annie replied.

Upon hearing mention of his mother, Groman straightened up and walked over to Annie and Victoria.

"Could you repeat the tune again?" Groman asked quietly.

Annie re-hummed the tune and was surprised to see Groman close his eyes and let out a long sigh.

"That is a tune I have not heard in a long time. It is 'The Hero's Hymn,'" he replied. "It is a song of mourning yet thankfulness for a hero who has given their life to save someone or something. Mother liked it because of its melody and hopeful message towards the end."

"Could...could you tell me the words?" Annie said quietly. "I don't remember any of them. Maybe hearing them will bring back other memories of Mother and Father."

Groman looked at Annie with a tear in his eye and closed his eyes again before he started.

> *"Rest now my warrior, the battle is now over.*
> *Thou hast fought well, and now are greatly honored.*
> *The sun rises, its rays cast o'er the battlefield.*
> *Friends assembled; their admiration garnered."*

As Groman continued to say the lines to the song, Victoria felt she should give the two siblings some time to themselves, went and sat next to Peregrine, and ate her breakfast in a hurry.

After the group was nearly done, two Kittrian guards walked over and saluted Groman. One was tall and wearing light armor, while the other was nearly Stephen's height and wearing a chest plate and visored helmet with the eye shield down.

"Commander Groman! I, Maku, am here as requested to lead you to the wanderer's staff," the taller one said.

"Very good, Maku. You will be going with Stephen, Windmere, Trakken, and Saralia to retrieve the artifact," Groman responded. He held out his hand, and the group watched in awe as the Empty Sword flew to its master's hand where he slid it into its sheath on his back.

At this, the other Kittrian cleared his throat and spoke up. "Commander, may I request permission to join Stephen's group?" the soldier inquired nervously, his voice echoing within the helmet.

Stephen stood up and walked over to the soldier, eyeing him up and down. "You sound familiar, soldier," he commented. "Do I know you?"

"Maybe this will help," the soldier wryly said. Before anyone could react, the soldier had drawn his sword and charged at Stephen, who had his own sword and shield at the ready in a moment. Their blades clashed once, twice, and then with a strange twist of the wrist, the soldier had managed to disarm Stephen. Stephen looked at his empty right hand before charging the soldier with his shield, ramming him off his feet and to the ground. The soldier laughed and held out his hand to Stephen, who quickly took it and helped him up.

"You! I knew it was you! To think, well over two years later, and you still got it!" Stephen said with a laugh. "How are you?"

"I am well, sir," the soldier replied as he retrieved Stephen's sword and returned it to its rightful owner. "I have earned the rank of lieutenant in the guard, thanks to your lessons back during your first visit."

"Your lessons and his tenacity," Groman said with a grim smile. "He has been a thorn in Falron's side for these last few years."

"I must admit I don't recall ever getting your name," Stephen said.

"Droven, sir," the soldier replied, holding out his hand. Stephen went in for the handshake, only to grip Droven's hand tightly and spin him around quickly. Droven gasped when he stopped, as Stephen had a dagger at his chest.

"I haven't taught you everything," Stephen playfully whispered in Droven's ear before laughing and releasing him.

Droven laughed, too, and soon, everyone was ready to go.

Stephen was on Trakken; Droven on Saralia, and Maku on Windmere, while Victoria was paired with Peregrine; Groman with Vulant, and Hannela and Annie were paired with the two Horiton.

Just before they left, Elder Gilder and Screnlon walked over to them.

"Are you all ready to go?" Screnlon asked.

"Yes, sir," Stephen said.

"Then, may The One Above protect and guide you on this journey," Elder Gilder replied. "May He show you the way to go and grant you success on this mission."

The group nodded their approval and quickly began gathering their gear and preparing to go.

As she climbed onto Peregrine's back, Victoria looked back at Stephen attempting to get situated on Trakken's back. "Watch their backs, Stephen!" she called out.

"You can be sure I will!" Stephen shouted back. "You all stay safe out there!"

"We'll do our best!" Annie replied as she held on to the Horiton's shoulders.

"Good luck to you all!" Vulant shouted before taking to the air. Peregrine and the Horiton quickly followed, with their riders hanging on as best they can.

"Is everybody ready?" Windmere asked.

"I have been ready since sunup," Saralia replied.

"Let us go find this artifact!" Droven said excitedly.

"Onward to Jeatut!" Maku shouted.

"Hold on tight, then!" Trakken said as he and his mother and sister took off at a gallop, nearly making Stephen lose his seating on Trakken's bare back.

After thundering through the camp and then across the bridge over the Green River, the group slowed to a trot to save their energy as they began to cross a wide-open prairie with the forest to their west.

As they continued on, Stephen tried to keep his focus on the task ahead and what their plan was should they find the artifact, but his mind started to wander again. He thought about Monaria's words and what he would do if he lost Groman or, worse, Victoria. At the mention of her name, his mind went further back to the events of last month: the police visit, the funeral, the legal mess, them selling the house and moving out, and now, this. He had tried to remain strong and resolute for Victoria, as he knew she needed someone to rely on. He was worried how either of them would respond to losing someone close to them again as they so nearly had last night with Belinda.

Suddenly, a voice broke his train of thought.

"How soon will we get there?" Droven asked.

"At this pace, we will arrive near sundown if we do not stop for rest," Saralia replied.

"Are you sure you can do it without stopping?" Maku asked.

"Well..." Saralia began.

"It would not be wise to do so," Windmere said, interrupting her daughter. "We do not know what may be waiting for us when we arrive, and having three fighters down to exhaustion is not a good idea should we run into a trap. I say we rest after high noon, so we are able to assist should trouble arise."

"I agree." Trakken added.

"What do you say, Stephen?" Windmere asked.

Stephen did not say anything, as he was once again lost in thought.

"Stephen?" Maku called out to him.

"Huh?" Stephen said confusedly.

"Shall we stop for a break partway through the journey so as to allow our friends to be rested enough to help us deal with any surprises, or shall we press on without stopping as to be able to reach the artifact sooner?" Droven asked.

"We are willing to press on should need be," Windmere added.

"I think stopping for a rest would be a good idea," Stephen replied.

"Agreed," Trakken echoed.

"We shall stop for a rest when we near the forest, then," Windmere said.

Stephen said nothing and remained silent as they pressed on throughout the day.

It was nearing late afternoon when they stopped for a rest under a small group of trees. Stephen was a short distance from the others, lying on his back with his eyes closed, trying to think about what he could do to help Victoria through all they had endured when he felt something heavy hit the ground next to his head. He instinctively rolled away and reached for his sword, only to see the tan hooves and legs of Saralia right in front of him. He sat up and looked at her, noticing her hands tucked into the front pockets of her reddish-brown shirt, her long blond hair and tail drifting in the gentle breeze, and the concerned look on her face.

"Did you need something?" Stephen asked her.

"Stephen, is everything alright?" Saralia replied. "You have seemed very distracted and distant ever since you returned. It is not like you, especially considering how you were on our last adventure."

Stephen looked at the ground and sighed. "I'm okay," he replied. "I just have some things on my mind right now."

"Would you like to talk about anything?" Saralia asked.

"Not really," Stephen answered.

"If you say so. I am willing to listen if you need someone to talk to."

Saralia began to turn away from Stephen, and he wondered if he should say anything about what had happened.

"Wait," he said quietly.

Saralia turned back to face him and then lay down in the grass next to him.

"What is troubling you, Stephen?" she asked again.

Stephen took a deep breath and looked Saralia in her brown eyes as his own began to well up with tears. Saralia's expression turned from concern to surprise when she saw his face. Stephen felt the tears running down his face as he began to get choked up with emotion. "My parents died last month," Stephen managed to say before the crying overcame him.

Before he knew it, Saralia had grabbed him and enveloped him in a tight hug. "I am so sorry, Stephen," she said softly. "I knew something was off with you, but I did not expect that."

She released Stephen from the hug, and he looked back at the ground. "They were killed in an accident on their way home from a wedding anniversary dinner. Someone else wasn't paying attention and hit them. The authorities came to our house and told us the news just as we were getting worried. Ever since then, we've been trying to put our lives back together, but things kept falling apart. A business partner of my dad's forcefully took over the company Dad had helped to start, and our parents hadn't written a proper will, so it took some weeks to get everything sorted out, and by that time, Tori and I were ready to just be done with everything. We had just finished moving into our Great Aunt Belinda's house when we got the message from Groman and came to Lulandal to help," Stephen said quietly.

"And how are you and Tori handling all this?" Saralia asked.

"Tori was really emotional through most of it. Recently, she has been doing better and been able to help me with the legal matters and such," Stephen answered.

"And what about you?"

Stephen paused and looked at Saralia with watery eyes. "Honestly, not so good. But it's okay; I've been trying to keep my mind off it and focus on taking care of my sister. She should have priority, right?"

Saralia put her hand on Stephen's shoulder as the two of them looked out over the grassy plains. "That is noble of you, but you are forgetting to take care of yourself. The pain you two are experiencing is like the pain of an open wound. If left alone, the wound will fester, and the flesh will cause you to become very ill. While it is certainly selfless for you to help your sister through this time, you need to let yourself mourn and treat this pain as well."

Stephen sniffed and looked at Saralia. "If I treat it, will the pain go away?"

Saralia gave Stephen a soft smile. "In time, the pain will lessen, but the scars never truly heal. Mother has never fully recovered from Father's death, and that was before I was even a foal. She always told me that she realized she will never be the same as she was while Father was alive, but she has learned to accept the change and live her life the way The One Above intends us to."

"And I know that I will see them again," Stephen added quietly.

"Indeed, we shall," Saralia replied.

Stephen looked behind him and noticed that Windmere and Trakken were up again and seemed ready to go. He stood up and was about to walk towards them when he felt Saralia pull him back. He turned around and saw she was back on her hooves but looking at him with a concerned expression.

"Are you sure you are ready?" she asked quietly.

"I'm as ready as I'll ever be," Stephen replied.

Saralia gave him another quick hug before releasing him again. "Alright. Would you like to ride with me for this stretch? I can keep a short distance from the others, and we can talk more if you want to."

"That would be nice," Stephen replied.

The two of them walked back to the group, and everyone gathered their things and prepared to leave once more. Stephen was a little embarrassed when Saralia spoke up and told the group that he and Droven would switch places, but nobody seemed to mind, and soon, they were off again.

Saralia was as good as her word, and she kept a stone's throw away from the others, allowing them some privacy. But even though the others wouldn't overhear them, Stephen and Saralia traveled in silence for some time, Stephen unsure of how much he should share despite his desperately wanting to talk to someone and Saralia not trying to pry more conversation out of him, enabling him to talk when he was ready.

Finally, after almost half an hour of silence between the two, Stephen spoke up: "Saralia, do you mind if I ask you a tough question?"

"Feel free to," she replied.

"Have you ever gotten a feeling that something bad was going to happen? I mean, like, something really bad?"

Saralia thought for a few moments before responding: "From time to time, but even then, the feelings are not always true. Why? Are you having one of those feelings?"

"I've had one ever since my second visit to this world."

"And what is this feeling telling you?"

"That something really bad is going to happen to Victoria here."

At this, Saralia stopped and looked back at Stephen. "Are you sure?!" she asked in surprise.

"I'm not completely certain, but ever since she was nearly paralyzed by The Shadowed One, I've always felt that she is going to get hurt again, and there is nothing I can do to stop it," he replied.

Saralia stood still for a few moments, contemplating her answer before she started walking again. "Stephen, that feeling you have is your desire to protect your sister; it is completely natural and not a bad thing. However, you must learn that we are in the hands of The One Above, and everything is in His control. If you live your life worrying about your sister, you will become a sorry fellow like Trakken over there."

"What?!" Stephen said in surprise.

"You have been gone for two years, so some things have happened. Trakken met someone and is completely enamored with her to the point where he is a nervous ninny when he is away from her, constantly worrying that she will be hurt before we get back," Saralia replied, raising her voice towards the end so that Trakken could overhear.

"What is that you are saying about me, my dear sister?" Trakken called back.

"That you are constantly worrying about your fiancée," Saralia replied playfully.

"Trakken? You're engaged?" Stephen asked.

"He most certainly is!" Windmere added.

At this, Trakken's face began to visibly redden, and he began to quicken his pace ahead of the rest of the group.

"She works with fine metals and gemstones. He commissioned a ring from her shop, saying it was for me, and when it was ready, he paid for it and then proposed," Saralia said with a chuckle. "Trinia knew it was for her, but she acted surprised all the same, and, of course, she said yes."

"I'm sure you're all excited for them," Stephen said.

"Indeed, we are," Windmere replied. "The two of them are a fine pair. It is a shame this war is going on, otherwise they may have been married sooner."

"Now, all Trakken does is worry about her back at camp. She is not a warrior by any means, so he goes out of his way to ensure her protection," Saralia said with a laugh.

"Why didn't he say anything about her or introduce us?" Stephen asked.

"He probably didn't want to overwhelm you upon your return. Also, you were not in any shape to meet her when you arrived at camp. It is hard to introduce someone who is unconscious," Saralia replied.

"That's true," Stephen said. He then leaned closer to Saralia and whispered in her ear: "Can you drop back a few paces? There's something else I need to talk about."

Saralia said nothing but slowed her pace again, allowing for more privacy.

"Saralia, when we visited Groman's tent last night, Monaria was there...she..." Stephen began.

"She had a vision, did she not?" Saralia quietly replied. "I assume that it was not good news."

"No..." Stephen softly said. "Her exact words were, 'Two shall stand, one shall fall. Two shall stand, one shall fall.' And when we guessed that she meant that one of us was going to die, she confirmed it before coming out of her trance."

Saralia froze abruptly, almost causing Stephen to fall off her back. She turned her head back to look at Stephen, her face white as a sheet. "You mean to tell me that you know one of you three heroes are supposedly going to perish before this battle is over?" she asked in shock.

"As far as we know, y-yes," Stephen replied shakily.

"Obviously, she did not say who, so we are left to guess until if or when the prophecy comes true," Saralia said as she began to walk again.

"If?" Stephen asked, perplexed.

"Monaria has become a good friend in the two years you have been back in your world; she confided in me that sometimes, her visions were not exactly how she said they were and occasionally wrong altogether. The leaders of the Flitnao say that it is due to her lack of experience and training of her mind," Saralia replied.

"So what you're saying is that she may be wrong, and we'll all live?" Stephen asked.

"I do not know. What I do know is that we can take precautions to make sure that all of you survive the coming battles."

"As much as I appreciate that, Saralia, I would ask that you promise me something."

"Of course."

"Should a time come where Victoria is in danger, and I ask you to protect her, you would do everything within your power to get her to safety."

"You have my word," Saralia said as she reached a hand back to Stephen, who clasped it tightly.

"I do not know if Monaria is right or not, but I want to make sure Victoria is kept safe if that is at all possible. After witnessing her injury at the hands of The Shadowed One, I don't ever want to see her get hurt again," Stephen said firmly.

"I will do what I am able. Until then, we should probably focus on the task at hand," Saralia replied as she shifted into a trot in order to catch up with the others.

"Right," Stephen replied.

*But how can I focus with the impending doom?*

# Chapter 5 Aerial Reconnaissance.

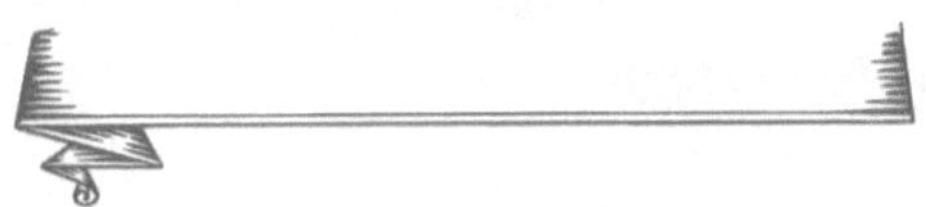

Victoria tightened her grip on Peregrine as she felt her stomach drop to her feet. As much as she felt she was ready for the g-forces upon her, the sudden acceleration and altitude change still got to her as she fought to keep her breakfast down. But within a few minutes, they were soaring high above the lands, heading towards the northern range. She looked back and barely caught a glimpse of the other group as they disappeared into the forest.

"Are you alright back there?"

Peregrine's voice broke the noise of air rushing past Victoria's ears.

"I'm fine!" Victoria replied quickly. She looked around and saw Vulant and Groman had taken point and were the tip of the "V" formation they had gotten into. She and Peregrine were on the right, and the Horiton and Annie were on the left, with the other Horiton and Hannela bringing up the rear.

"We are about two thousand feet up at this point!" Peregrine called out. "If we keep going higher, the air will thin, and we will have more problems."

"This is high enough!" Groman called back. "Once we arrive at the mountains, we need to find that shrine or temple quickly before Falron does."

"Right!" Vulant answered.

"Leave that to us!" one of the Horiton called out.

"We were told it was in the center of four peaks," the other added.

"That's a good start!" Victoria said hopefully.

Within two hours, the group had arrived over the mountains and started to circle as they climbed ever higher.

"Where shall we look first?" Vulant called out.

"I say we look west!" Groman answered.

"Any objections?!" Vulant shouted.

"None here!" Annie replied.

"Let's go!" Victoria added.

Hannela and the Horiton simply nodded, and the group began to soar westward, slowly scanning the mountain peaks to their right. Victoria remembered when she, Annie, Saralia, and several of their other friends had climbed that same range two years prior. She recalled being caught in the avalanche, their rescue by the Ibexians, and the trials they had to complete in order to be allowed to hunt down a monster in order to leave, then the monster attacking the Ibexians and their party hunting and killing the beast anyways. Back then, the mountains seemed very daunting, and even now, as they were flying by them, they still seemed massive with their snow-covered peaks; some of which were nearly twice as high as they were flying.

"Does anyone see anything yet?!" Annie called out.

"Just snow!" the Horiton in the rear called back.

"Remember to look for the four peaks!" Vulant called back.

"What four peaks?" Hannela replied. "There are literally thousands of them in this range."

"We just need to keep searching!" Groman shouted. "We will find it eventually!"

The eight of them pressed on as they flew westward. As they flew, they switched places, with Victoria and Peregrine taking point; Annie behind them and to their left; Groman and Vulant behind them and on their right, with Hannela behind him. Soon, they could see the Dusky Sea on the horizon and still had not seen anything resembling the four peaks that had been mentioned.

"We are running out of mountains!" Peregrine shouted.

"Then, we turn around and go back over them again!" Groman replied quickly. "We must not lose this artifact to the enemy!"

After flying over the remaining mountains, the group wheeled about and started going over their own tracks, desperately trying to find any sign of the shrine. Soon, they did see something, but it was not what they wanted to see.

"Storm ahead!" Vulant called out.

"Do we turn back to Areiop?" Peregrine asked.

"No, we should look for a cave to take shelter in until the storm passes!" Groman called back. "The more time we can spend searching for the shrine, the better!"

Everyone agreed, and soon, they spotted a cave tucked away between some mountain peaks. After landing and hurrying inside, they used the remains of a tree that must have been pushed inside by an avalanche to start a fire as the storm howled outside. The Horiton stood guard near the entrance, while Vulant, Peregrine, and Hannela looked around the cave, using some torches. Groman, Annie, and Victoria all sat on stones around the fire, trying to stay warm.

Then, Groman's voice broke the silence: "Victoria, Annie has told me what you and Stephen have gone through in the recent weeks. I just wanted to say I am truly sorry for your loss. If I had known, I would have treated your arrival with a little more kindness than what I did. I am sorry for my coldness towards you."

"It's alright, Groman," Victoria answered. "Honestly, I feel like you've almost been through more than us."

Groman sighed and looked at the campfire. "Perhaps, but I lost my parents when I was much younger. I have had time to heal from those wounds. Yours are still fresh and raw. You need to let them heal; not enter a battlefield of sorrow and mourning," he replied.

"Tori, how is Stephen doing?" Annie asked quietly. "He hasn't spoken much to me recently."

"He has been trying to keep his emotions in check and not show them in public," Victoria answered with a sigh. "And I can tell that is hurting him."

"Why is he doing that?" Groman asked.

"I think it's because he wants to be a 'rock' for me: someone I can lean on when things are tough," Victoria answered.

"Have you needed someone like that?" Groman asked.

"A few times. I'll admit I was very emotional for the first week or so. But I'm doing better, now. As for Stephen, he just doesn't see that he needs help too. He is intent on making sure he's here for me when he also needs someone to be there for him."

"Have you been able to 'be there' for him or made him aware of your concern for him?" Annie asked.

"I don't know. I've tried to be. I'm not sure if he thinks he needs the help, or if he does, he hasn't really said anything to me."

"Sometimes, all you have to do is ask," Annie said quietly. "Knowing the offer is there may be enough. That's what Belinda did for me when I was getting accustomed to your world."

Victoria pondered what Annie had said for a few minutes. She realized that she hadn't really asked Stephen how he had been doing in the last few weeks. She had just been happy to have him to cling to when she was going through a more emotional moment. And now that they were back in Lulandal, facing another powerful enemy, she decided she needed to talk to him as soon as she saw him again in person.

"The storm shows no sign of letting up!" one of the Horiton called out from the entrance. "It would be wise to make camp here for the night."

"Is the cave clear of possible danger?!" Groman called back.

"There is no threat here," Hannela's voice came directly from behind Victoria, causing her to jump off her rock and draw her blades. Before she knew what was going on, Hannela was on her back, barely holding off Victoria's claws with her own Katar.

"Victoria! Snap out of it!" Annie's screams echoed in Victoria's ears, and she quickly jumped back, allowing Hannela to jump to her paws.

"I am so sorry, Hannela," Victoria said quickly. "I don't know what came over me."

"It is alright, my friend," Hannela said breathlessly. "I should not have startled you."

"All the same, I nearly took your head off!" Victoria gasped. She quickly put her claws back in their holsters and backed away.

"True, I will admit your reflexes in that moment astounded me. I have never seen someone move so fast," Hannela replied.

"You were seated one moment and then slashing wildly the next," Annie said.

"Our kind naturally has very quick reflexes, and while Father's is quick enough to catch arrows out of the air, yours appear to be faster. We will have to spar when we return to camp; I am interested to see just how fast you are!" Hannela said excitedly.

"I...I don't think that would be a good idea," Victoria said hesitantly as she sat down by the fire again.

"Why not?" Hannela asked.

"I don't want to hurt you. When you surprised me, I didn't really know what I was doing when I attacked you."

Hannela sat down next to Victoria, her yellow eyes standing out from the shadow cast by her hood.

"I understand. It is hard to retain control when your body wants to take over. Father has helped me tame that side of myself, so I can be in complete control all of the time. Before you act, take a deep breath and focus on what is going on around you, see what is and is not a threat, and then act on that knowledge," Hannela said quietly.

"Take a breath and focus? I'll try to remember that," Victoria replied.

Hannela purred her approval and then laid down near the fire and was soon asleep. The rest of the group soon followed, with men taking turns keeping watch, while the storm raged outside.

It was near sunset when the Trodontians and their riders arrived at their destination. It was the ruins of what looked like an old house that had been swallowed up by the forest. The roof was long gone and windows shattered. All that was left were the stone walls and wooden door that had nearly rotted off its hinges.

When they saw the house, the riders dismounted, and all six approached cautiously on foot or hoof.

"Alright, we're here. Where is the artifact, Maku?" Stephen asked.

"Well...I am ashamed to admit I do not know," Maku replied. The rest of the group stopped in their tracks and looked at him. "I do apologize for my lack of information, but my father had only shown me where this ruin was located and said that the artifact was somewhere inside."

"So we merely need to search the ruins?" Saralia asked. "That seems simple enough."

"Oh! There was one more thing: My father said something about the morning light helping us find our way or something like that," Maku added quickly. "Unfortunately, it has been a long time since he brought me here, so I do not recall what exactly he meant."

"Well, I suggest we look over the ruins and see what we can find in what little light we have remaining. Some of you should begin setting up camp, while the others search," Windmere said.

"I shall go looking for some food," Saralia said, stringing her bow.

"Droven and I can set up camp," Trakken added.

"I shall help with the camp as well," Maku said.

"I guess that leaves me and Windmere to search the house," Stephen said.

"Good luck!" Saralia said as she disappeared into the forest shadows as quietly as someone with hooves for feet could.

Stephen pulled out a pocket flashlight he had, and Windmere quickly made a torch from some dry wood she found; together, they began to search the house. It was rather large compared to most Kittrian buildings Stephen had seen before, and its construction of stone was also somewhat unusual to the Kittrian way of home building. Very little of anything resembling furniture remained, and there seemed to be no special room or vault where one might hide an ancient artifact of great power.

"Have you seen anything yet?" Stephen asked as he examined more stone walls covered with moss and vines.

"I have not. This ruin is extremely barren of anything one would expect from a large home like this," Windmere's response came from the next room over.

"Who do you think lived here?"

"Hard to guess. The rooms are large enough for even my kind to walk around without much issue, but with it being roughly a few miles from a Kittrian village, one may expect it to have been built for them by them."

"Maybe it was a hunting lodge? A place for hunters to replenish their supplies or sell their trophies?" Stephen suggested after he spotted what looked to be a skull with four horns attached to a rotted wooden board.

"That could be a possibility," Windmere said from behind Stephen, making him jump. Windmere chuckled and stomped a front hoof on the ground, making little noise. And as if to prove her point, Windmere reared up on her hind legs, towering over Stephen, then came back down with only a soft *thump* and the jingle of her weapons and gear making any sound. "The floorboards have all rotted away, leaving moss and dirt in their place. Even I can be silent here."

Stephen let out a short chuckle and tried to walk past Windmere, but she turned to block his path.

"Saralia told me about what happened to your family. I am so sorry for your loss," she said quietly.

Stephen felt his eyes begin to water again as Windmere quickly noticed and hugged him tightly. "Thank you, Windmere," he replied.

"When this is over, please know my family and I are here for you if you need anything."

Stephen silently nodded his thanks, and the two of them exited the ruins as it was now completely dark.

They made their way to where the rest of the group had set up camp just as Saralia returned carrying two deer-like animals. They were about the same size as whitetail deer from Earth but oddly had tusks like a boar and three clawed toes instead of hooves.

"I have returned with fresh brown tooth meat," she said proudly.

"My favorite!" Droven said excitedly.

After they had cooked and eaten their dinner, Stephen stood up and looked at the group. "If you don't mind, I'd like to be alone for a little bit. I'll be nearby in the ruins. I'll call if I need help," he said quietly.

"Alright, just be careful," Windmere replied.

As Stephen walked away into the darkness, the others soon drifted off to sleep while Trakken took first watch.

After a few hours, Stephen returned to the campsite.

"Are you alright, Stephen?" Trakken asked quietly.

"Honestly, I'm doing better than I was before," Stephen replied. "I'll take over on watch now for you."

Trakken nodded his agreement and settled down to sleep.

"Hey, Trakken," Stephen whispered.

Trakken didn't say anything but looked at Stephen.

"I just wanted to say...thank you. You and your family have been so good to me and Victoria while we've been here, and we really haven't done anything to repay you," Stephen said quietly.

Trakken stood up and walked over to Stephen. "Nothing?" he whispered. "You have saved our world from The Shadowed One as well as returning not once but twice to aid us against Falron. That is far from nothing, my friend."

Stephen pondered what his friend said and then looked at Trakken in the eyes. "Thank you Trakken," he replied. "And one more thing: Don't be afraid to introduce us to new friends or family when we come to visit or help out. Your fiancée sounds like a great person, and I'm looking forward to meeting her."

Trakken grinned and patted Stephen's shoulder. "That she is, my friend. That she is," he said.

The sun pouring into the cave quickly woke the travelers from their slumber, and they were soon back into the air heading east and searching for where the artifact might be hidden.

"Anything yet?" Annie called out to the group as she and a Horiton had taken the lead in the formation.

"Nothing to the south," Groman replied.

Victoria peered to her left and spotted four mountain peaks all arranged in a diamond formation. She quickly waved her arm to get everyone's attention. "Wait! I think I see four peaks!" she called out.

"Where?" Vulant asked.

"Up ahead and to our left!" Victoria replied.

"It is almost within the Ice Dwarves' territory," Peregrine replied.

The group began to descend and fly around the peaks, looking for anything that stood out.

Then, Groman's voice called out, echoing around the mountains: "There! I see an entrance of some sort!"

The group quickly flew over to it and landed just in front of it. It was a moderate stone doorway that had looked like it had been through several rough centuries. It was cracked, and parts of the stonework were crumbling away. On the ground in front of it were the decaying remnants of two ancient wooden doors and, to the group's horror, the partial remains of a winged skeleton.

"Well, we aren't the first people here, are we?" Victoria commented.

Groman examined the skeleton and pulled a small metal object out of the back of the skull. "I would say this fellow has been here for many years. As for what killed him, this dart seemed to have done him in."

"May I see that?" Hannela asked.

Groman handed her the object, and she held it to her nose and sniffed. She fleetingly wrinkled her nose and flicked the dart into the rocks below them.

"Poison," she said quickly, "a common one at that but still lethal even when sitting for many years. It is made from the yellow bloatfish. Father and I have built up an immunity to it, but it would be best for us all to be cautious. As you had suspected, there may very well be traps inside."

"It was not something I wanted to be right about," Groman said with disdain. "Hannela, could you take the lead? You know more about traps than any of us."

"It is why you brought me, is it not?" Hannela purred before lighting a torch and silently walking inside.

The rest of the group lit torches of their own and followed the young ninja at a safe distance. Soon, they rounded a bend in the tunnel and were quickly stopped by Hannela holding up her hand and crouching down.

"Stop. The trap is here," she said quickly.

"How did you know that?" one of the Horiton asked.

"I can smell the poison," Hannela said confidently. She then picked up a stone and threw it into the tunnel. When it landed, a *click* and a whistling sound was heard. Hannela turned back to the group and smiled. "I rest my case." She purred.

"Okay, so how do we get through that without getting killed?" Victoria asked.

"There are several ways," Hannela replied. "We can continue to throw rocks into the tunnel until the traps have spent their darts, though we do now know how many there are, and that may take a long time. We could return to camp, gather up some shields, and use them for protection, though there may be some traps to counter such an approach. We can give up and simply return back to camp empty handed. Or...." Hannela took a cautious step forward with her right leg, feeling the stone floor with her paw. After feeling around, she placed her weight on it, and nothing happened. "I can try and press on and then figure out a way to disarm this trap, so the rest of you can follow."

"And if you cannot disarm it?" Annie asked.

"Then, I will retrieve the artifact and return to you as quickly as I can," Hannela said calmly.

"Very well, then. You may proceed," Groman said.

Hannela stretched out her left leg and felt around until she felt a solid stone under her paw and then took the step forward. Each step was very slow and meticulous, and everyone held their breath as Hannela felt the stones under her paws before taking a step. After nearly ten minutes of her slow advance, she froze in place. Her yellow eyes widened with fear.

"What's wrong?!" Victoria called out.

"I have put too much pressure on a trapped stone," Hannela said breathlessly. "Should I move another hair, a dart will hit my body."

"But you've built an immunity to that toxin, right?" Annie asked.

"It would still be very painful and take me out of any possible fight, let alone be able to proceed."

"Hold on, I'm coming to help you," Victoria said. She moved to take a step forward, only to see Hannela's tail pointing at her, its metal tip glinting in the torchlight.

"Do not move," Hannela said firmly. "I have an idea, but I need absolute silence for better concentration."

Victoria took a step back and watched as Hannela moved her tail down towards the stone her right paw was on. She slowly applied pressure with her prehensile tail and then lifted her paw and placed it on the safe stone it had been on prior. She crouched down and then jumped swiftly up and twisted her body so that it would be parallel to the ceiling. Her tail wasn't long enough to keep pressure on the trapped stone, and it released its dart, which pinged off the metal tail tip and into the stone floor. Hannela then used her claws to cling to the roots and stones in the roof and then began to crawl along it.

"Incredible!" one of the Horiton muttered.

"That's why we brought her," Victoria said with a smile.

Hannela kept crawling upside down on the roof for another twenty feet before stopping and sniffing the air. She then released the claws on her paws and hung from the ceiling by her hands. Seeing she could reach the floor, she used her long black tail to feel it and, finding it safe, dropped soundlessly to the ground. She quickly looked around the stone walls, found a loose stone, and dug it out with her claws. After she did so, she reached inside and swiped at something, making a loud snapping sound. She then turned back to the group, her yellow eyes brighter than ever.

"I did it!" she said excitedly. "I have cut the tripwires; the passageway should be safe to cross, now."

"I shall go first," Groman said. He slowly took a step forward, then another; then another. Hannela had been true to her word.

Soon, the rest of the group had crossed the passageway, and around a corner, they found what they had been looking for. It was a large round room with a fairly high ceiling, and there in the center of it was a large stone pedestal, on top of which was a strange item. It was black in color and looked like two goat horns that had been fastened together at their tips and spreading out in a "V" formation.

"Is that it?!" Annie asked excitedly.

"The horn of the Horiton," Groman answered.

"Well, this seemed rather easy," Victoria said.

"For you," Hannela growled.

"Sorry!" Victoria quickly apologized.

"Our ancestors likely did not think anyone could pass that trap and thus did not add any more safeguards," one of the Horiton added.

"That makes sense," Annie said.

"Well, should we just take it?" the other Horiton asked.

Before the group could answer, a loud beeping noise filled the room.

"What is that?!" Vulant shouted.

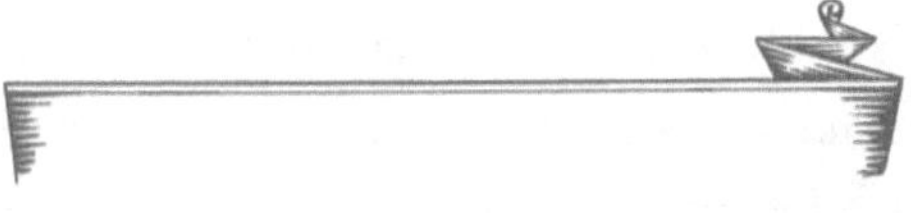

# Chapter 6 Surprises.

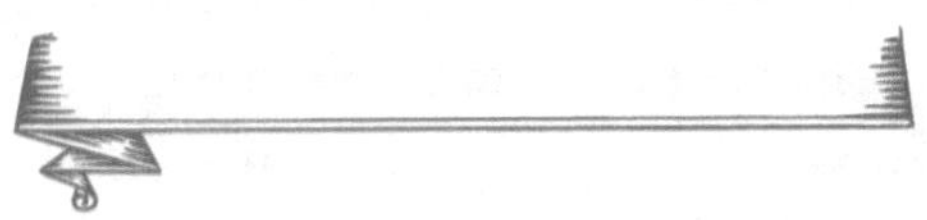

Stephen awoke to the sunlight just coming through the treetops. He noticed that everyone else was on their feet and looking around the ruined building again. Maku especially was running around looking at every stone or rotten wood wall that was left standing.

"The morning sun should reveal the clue!" Maku kept repeating as he ran.

Stephen got up and wandered into the ruins. They looked much less ominous in the daylight, and he could clearly see that they were in much worse shape than he thought.

That was when he noticed a beam of light coming through the treetops. He followed it to the canopy and spotted what looked like a lens suspended from the trees by old cords of rope. It was so high up, he wouldn't have otherwise noticed it unless he'd known it existed. He looked at where the beam of light was going and saw it resting on a stone wall that seemed to be up against a large tree.

"Maku! Over here!" Stephen called out.

Maku was there in seconds and stared at the wall in excitement. "That must be it! We found it!" he shouted energetically.

Soon, the rest of the group had joined them and were inspecting the wall.

"I do not see any sign of a secret passageway," Trakken said as he felt the mossy stones.

"Maybe it is below us?" Saralia suggested. She motioned for everyone else to back away before rearing up on her hind legs and then coming down with her full weight. When nothing happened, she tried jumping in place a few times but to no avail.

"There has to be something here," Windmere said. She trotted over to the wall and pushed it, but it didn't even budge.

"Wait," Maku said as he pushed past Windmere. He knelt down and pointed at a small hole in the stonework towards the bottom of the wall. It was barely big enough to stick a ballpoint pen in.

"Is that a keyhole?" Stephen asked.

"I do not know. But if it is, we will need the key," Maku said.

"I suppose you do not have it?" Droven asked.

"No," Maku replied dejectedly.

"Well, maybe it is around here somewhere," Windmere said.

"Would it be made of metal?" Stephen asked.

"I would assume so," Droven replied.

"Well, I know it sounds silly, but maybe if we all feel around with our feet, we might find it under the moss and dirt, especially if you're wearing metal shoes," Stephen said while looking at his Trodontian friends.

"Wait!" Saralia said quickly. "Trakken, do you still have that gift you made for Trinia?"

Trakken turned a little red and looked at the ground. "Yes. I have not had a good time to give this to her." He pulled out a long wooden rod with what looked like a piece of shiny black stone attached to the end of it. He pointed it at Stephen's sword and the blade began to float into the air towards the stone.

"A magnet! That's a great idea and a neat tool, Trakken," Stephen said to compliment his friend.

"Is that what you call them in your world?" Trakken asked as he began to sweep the magnet over the soil. "I call them metal seekers. They are quite hard to find, and I had fashioned a tool like this for myself to use while I am working at the forge. As we cannot bend down easily to reach something we drop, so these are quite useful. I made this one for Trinia, as she also routinely works with metals, and as they are often smaller pieces, one of these would benefit her greatly."

Within a matter of moments, a click was heard, and Trakken lifted the magnet to reveal a clump of dirt with something shiny sticking out of it. He picked it off the magnet and rubbed the dirt away to reveal a long silver key.

"Well, that may be it," Maku said. "I wonder what it was doing over here instead of being in my family's possession?"

"Who knows?" Saralia replied. "Keys are easy things to lose."

"True," Stephen added.

Trakken handed the key to Maku, who knelt down and inserted the key into the lock. As he struggled to turn the ancient key, Stephen heard a twig snap from behind him. He turned and looked where the sound had come from, only to see nothing.

"You heard it too?" Saralia's voice came from behind him.

"Yeah," Stephen replied. "I'd guess it was a wild animal or something, but it'd be hard to tell with how quietly you can walk around these ruins."

"It was probably a Grelout or a Spineback. They would probably love hunting in a place like this."

"I'd agree with you if I knew what you were talking about," Stephen replied with a laugh.

Saralia gave him a playful shove and then sighed. "Stephen, how are you doing this morning?" she asked quietly.

"I'm doing better. Thank you," Stephen replied calmly.

"I am glad to hear it."

Just then, a loud *click* was heard, followed by the creaks and groans of an ancient door opening.

"I got it!" Maku cried excitedly.

Saralia and Stephen spun around and saw a hidden door open up within the stone wall. It led into a passageway that had been carved into the tree and down into the earth.

"At least it is not a set of stairs," Windmere said as she looked down into the passageway.

"Will you three be alright going down the ramp?" Stephen asked his Trodontian companions.

"We will manage," came Trakken's reply.

"I will stay outside and keep watch," Maku said.

"Are you sure?" Stephen asked.

"Yes," Maku replied. "My family are sworn to protect this place; I am merely following in their footsteps."

"Alright. Please let us know if you see anything out of the ordinary," Windmere said before she slowly made her way down the stone ramp into a dark passageway.

Maku nodded and watched as Stephen, Trakken, Droven, and Saralia all made their way down into the darkness below.

Once the ground leveled off, they lit some torches that had been set into rings on the wall and used them to light their way. It was not a long passageway, but it made several turns right and left before it opened up into a large room. Stephen and Trakken noticed more torches set into the walls and used theirs to light them. Once those were lit, the group quickly began to light the other torches they saw around the room until all were ignited. Once they could see their surroundings better, they noticed racks of weapons along the walls as well as various tools on workbenches.

Trakken picked up a crossbow up off a hook on the wall and examined it. "The string deteriorated a long time ago, but the weapon itself is not in too bad a shape," he commented.

"These weapons could equip a small army. It is a shame we did not bring a wagon with us," Windmere added.

"Which one is the artifact?" Droven asked.

"Maku called it a staff, so maybe start by looking for any of those?" Stephen replied.

"There are several here to pick from," Saralia said.

"Well, let's just look them over and see if we can figure it out," Stephen said.

The group looked around, gathered up all the staves they could find, and put them on a table in the middle of the room. Many were ornately carved or had intricate patterns etched into them. A few were made of metal and had pointed tips like a spear. One in particular had a miniature lantern set into the top of it.

"Did anyone get a jolt from one of these?" Stephen asked.

"No," Trakken replied.

"Not me," Saralia added.

"I felt nothing," Windmere said.

"No pain here," Droven replied.

"So which one is the one we are looking for?" Stephen asked in a frustrated tone.

"Maybe we should send for Maku and see if he can remember which one it is," Droven said.

At that moment something was sent rolling into the room, causing the party to go silent. They watched in horror as Maku's helmet rolled over to a table leg where it came to rest. Stephen felt sick as he saw blood coming from it; even with its visor down he knew what was still inside. But before he could really react to that sight, he heard footsteps enter the room. He and his Trodontian friends turned to see a cloaked figure enter the armory.

"I'm afraid that Maku isn't able to answer any questions right now. He was unable to get 'ahead' of the situation topside, though you'll be touched to know he did try to warn you. I had to move quickly before he could give you a 'head's up,'" the figure said with a laugh.

"Falron!" Stephen shouted while drawing his sword and freeing his shield from his back. The others quickly drew their own weapons and stood ready to fight.

The figure pulled down his hood to reveal a gaunt human face with glowing purple eyes and stringy white hair. "So you do remember me? Good. I was thinking you had run off and forgotten me after our first meeting so long ago," Falron said with another laugh.

"How could I forget what you did to my sister and friends?" Stephen said as he readied himself for an attack.

"Oh, those were merely parlor tricks compared to what I can do now. Especially after you let me have the staff," Falron said.

"Over my dead body," Windmere said coldly.

"Funny, that's what your friend outside said too." Falron chuckled. His eye color switched from purple to red as he raised his hands towards the group.

"Hit the dirt!" Stephen yelled as a torrent of flame roared from Falron's fingertips, dousing the wooden shelves along the walls and setting them ablaze. Stephen felt the heat as he looked behind him to make sure his friends were alright. Droven was fine and hiding under a table; the Trodontians had also gotten on the ground, but Saralia wasn't quite fast enough.

"My hair!" she shrieked as she frantically put out her smoldering locks.

Falron laughed as his eyes went from red to purple. He raised his hands and summoned three shadow Amronian warriors.

"My friends here should keep you busy until I find the staff. Have fun, boys!" Falron shouted to the shadows, and they shrieked and attacked.

Stephen leapt to his feet and rushed two of the shadows that were closest to him; using his shield as a battering ram, he plowed right through them and then quickly checked to see where the third one was. He felt a wave of relief when he saw Droven quickly dispatch it with his own blade as the Trodontians were struggling to their feet.

Falron was looking over the table they had left all the staves on and grabbing each one before throwing it into the now-blazing shelves along the walls. Before Stephen could stop him, Droven rushed towards the table and grabbed an ornately carved staff that he had put there earlier.

Falron looked at him in surprise before smiling with a twisted look. "Oh, you found it for me! How nice," he said with a laugh.

"You will have to t-take it from my corpse," Droven said. He was clearly attempting to be brave, but there was an unmistakable quiver in his voice.

Stephen sprinted over to the two of them as fast as he could as he heard Falron's chilling reply.

"No sooner said than done," Falron said with a grin before his eyes changed to red again, and he sent a torrent of flame at Droven.

Stephen jumped in front of Droven, using his shield to block the flames. He could feel the metal bracing begin to melt and the sturdy wood start burning, but he stood his ground. Even though it felt like hours, the flames only lasted for a few seconds, and the unrelenting heat let up. Stephen looked over the melted edge of the shield and tried to see where Falron went before hearing Droven shout in a panic.

"He has my leg! He is under the table!"

Stephen quickly brought his sword down in an attempt to cut Falron's arms off, but Falron was just fast enough and quickly pulled back. By this time, the Trodontians were on their feet, and Saralia was loosing arrow after arrow at Falron.

"Perhaps I am outmatched. Just this once, I'll let you live for now!" Falron called back as he sprinted out of the chamber.

"After him!" Windmere shouted as the Trodontians broke into a full gallop. Droven and Stephen raced after them as best they could.

Soon, they reached the outside and looked around, only to see no sign of Falron.

"Did we lose him?" Stephen panted.

"It would appear so," Trakken said quietly.

"At least we got the staff away from him," Droven said as he spun it around in his hand.

"Be careful! We do not know what it can do," Windmere said.

Just then, a beeping sound came from Stephen's sleeve.

"What is that?" Saralia asked.

"Just my watch. It's probably Victoria wanting to check in on us," Stephen said as he pulled his sleeve back and pressed a button on the device. A hologram of Victoria appeared on top of his watch in front of the surprised group. Droven and Trakken jumped back, Windmere dropped her sword, and Saralia reared up on her hind legs.

"By The One Above! What is that?!" Windmere shouted.

Victoria's image laughed and looked at Stephen, who pressed a button, and the projection was then sent to the ground in front of him, so it looked like Victoria was standing there. "Sorry for the surprise. Stephen should have told you about this beforehand," she said, giving Stephen a quick look. "This is a device that our father designed back on our world to help people communicate over long distances."

"Fascinating," Windmere said as she pulled her sword out of the ground.

"It looks like you are here with us," Saralia added as she stepped forward and tried to touch the hologram, only to have her hand pass through it.

Victoria laughed again and then pressed a button on her watch. Suddenly, the figures of Annie and Groman were beside her as well as what looked like a round chamber. Annie waved at the group before walking out of the picture. Victoria looked behind the group and raised an eyebrow.

"What's with the smoke? Did everything go alright?" she asked.

"Falron showed up," Stephen answered, showing off his melted shield before throwing it aside.

"Oh no. Is everyone alright?"

"Maku was killed in the line of duty. He had volunteered to stay behind on watch, while we went inside to search for the artifact. Falron ambushed him and killed him before attacking us."

"Maku is gone?" Groman asked.

"Sadly, yes," Windmere replied.

"Then, who's that behind Droven?!" Victoria asked, nearly shouting at them.

The group spun around to see Falron was behind them and grasping for the staff. Droven tried to pull it away, but Falron was able to grab the bottom tip of it.

"At last, the power that was contained within this staff is mine!" He laughed as the staff began to lose its color where he had grabbed it. Droven kicked Falron in the gut, and he staggered back. The part of the staff Falron had been holding broke off with a snap before turning into dust and blowing away in the wind.

"You're too late, boy!" Falron said as his eyes turned green. Suddenly, he vanished only to reappear on top of Trakken's back. "I have the power now!"

Trakken bucked as hard as he could but before his legs even left the ground, Falron had vanished again.

"Victoria! Get that artifact and get to safety, now!" Stephen shouted as he drew his sword and frantically looked for Falron. He heard a scream from behind him and spun around just in time to block Falron's sword swinging for his midsection.

"Someone, grab the horn!" Victoria's voice came from the holographic image as Stephen pushed Falron back, only to have him vanish again.

"Where did he go?" Saralia said. She held her scimitars in a ready position.

What was heard next sent the whole group into shock.

"He's over here!" Victoria's voice screamed through the watch.

The chamber had turned into chaos in mere moments. Falron suddenly appeared in the midst of the group, laughing manically. Everyone had gone for their weapons, but he had vanished again.

"Where is he?" Hannela growled as she quickly scanned the room.

"Right here, kitty," Falron said with a chuckle.

Everyone turned to see him in the center of the room reaching for the horn.

"No!" Victoria shouted. She rushed towards Falron and attacked, her claws narrowly missing his hand and separating the horns. The freed horn fell to the ground, and the one in Falron's grip seemed to dull for a moment but then returned to its normal color.

"I must say, young lady, that was exceptionally quick of you," Falron said. "But I must be off. Bye!"

And just like that, he was gone again.

Everyone scanned the room, and when they realized they were safe, Victoria looked back at the hologram of Stephen to see he had been watching the whole thing.

"You good?" Stephen asked.

"We are well," Groman said as he placed The Empty Sword back into its sheath on his back.

"Falron isn't back with you?" Stephen asked.

"He is gone for now," Hannela said after sniffing the air.

"He got the horn, didn't he?" Stephen quietly asked.

"Part of it," Peregrine said.

Just then, Stephen's eyes widened, and he pointed behind Victoria. She turned and saw Annie was picking up the remaining horn.

"I felt I needed to get it off the floor," Annie said quietly.

"Well, this has been a crazy day," Stephen said. "We need to regroup and figure out our next move, as well as if we can figure out if those artifacts still work."

"We will rendezvous back at the encampment," Vulant said.

"Sounds like a good plan to me," Windmere replied.

"Be safe," Groman said.

"We will do our best, sir!" Droven said with a salute.

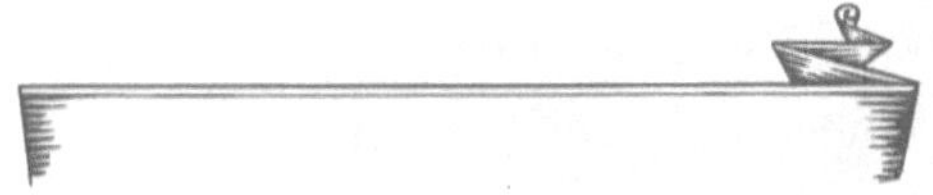

# Chapter 7. Time to find out.

Victoria's group landed in the camp in the early evening hours. Hannela had tried to talk Victoria into sparring with her again, but she had declined, saying she was too tired after the day's encounter. Now, she lay in her hammock as the young cat ninja slept soundly above her. She wondered what was coming over her: Twice now, she had reacted to things faster than she had thought even possible. Was she really that good? Her martial arts instructors had often complimented her reflexes and agility, but this? Reacting faster than the eye could track?

*This isn't possible; it can't be done.*

It seemed to be connected to her claws. The power she felt while holding them was similar to the broken gauntlets back when she used them during her first adventure. But they weren't some ancient artifacts, were they?

Before she could think about it some more, sleep took hold.

She was awoken by the sunlight beginning to come through the trees. She got out of the hammock and reached for her claws. She picked them up and felt a small surge of energy go through her body. She swung them around and didn't feel any different.

"Ready to spar, now?" Hannela's voice purred from the upper hammock.

"Not right now," Victoria said quickly. "Stephen and his group will be here soon. We need to be ready to discuss our next move as soon as we can."

Hannela said nothing but nodded her agreement as she nimbly jumped out her hammock and flipped over Victoria, landing on her paws like a trained gymnast. "You are just scared of losing to me," the cat purred before leaving the tent.

*No,* Victoria thought. *I'm scared of what I might do to you if I were to try.*

After a quick breakfast of bread and vegetables, Victoria walked to the edge of the camp where her brother and his group were likely to arrive. She leaned up against a tree and sighed.

"Do you see them yet?" A young woman's voice came from behind her.

"Not yet," Victoria replied before turning around to see who was speaking. She was surprised to see a young Trodontian woman walking towards her. She was just shy of six feet tall and had a slender build. She had light skin and long curly walnut brown hair she had up in a sort of ponytail, and her long horse tail was the same color, with a few small braids woven into it. Her face was delicate, and her hazel eyes sparkled in the early light. Her horse half was also a walnut brown with large white tobiano splotches and white hooves to match. She wore a brown and bronze shirt and had a sort of backpack on her back. She also had a large, jeweled pendant around her neck, feathered earrings, and a ring on the ring finger of her left hand.

"Hello! Who are you?" Victoria asked.

"My name is Trinia," the Trodontian replied. "I am a worker of gemstones and fine metals by trade. I also happen to be Trakken's fiancée," she added with a smile.

"Is that so?" Victoria asked. "I never heard anything about his engagement."

Trinia swished her long tail and looked out at the forest again. "He did not want to add to the chaos of your sudden arrival. We felt it would be best for you to find out later when you were accustomed to our world again," she replied quietly.

Victoria walked up to where Trinia was standing and held out her hand. "Well, it is nice to meet you now Trinia. I am Victoria," she said as Trinia took her hand and shook it. "You may call me Tori if you'd like."

Trinia smiled before she looked back at the forest.

Victoria looked at her new friend over again and realized something. "Is it just me, or are you a bit shorter than the normal Trodontian?" she mused.

Trinia turned to face her with an annoyed look. "I was born this way. Mother said it was due to my being a twin and very weak at birth."

"I'm sorry, I didn't mean to insult you," Victoria replied quickly.

"I forgive you. It is just that it is what most of my people see first. They do not always see who I am. Just my size," Trinia said with a sigh. "Then, there was my Trakken. He said something similar when we first met but mentioned how useful it must be being as small as I am. I will admit we realized our mutual respect and love for each other soon after."

"He does seem the pragmatic type."

"Yes, but he is so much more than that. Even his sister notices how he has changed after we met; his constant wish to protect me from everything and everyone who means me harm. He sometimes treats me like a foal, but, as someone whose life has been a struggle from a young age, I appreciate the care and love he has for me."

"Does he get along with your family?"

Trinia sighed again before pawing the ground with a front hoof. "My mother loved him like her own foal before she was killed during the siege of Prariat. He has taken extra care of me ever since then. While we will never meet in this lifetime, I am certain my twin sister would have loved Trakken too."

"I'm so sorry for you, Trinia." Victoria paused and looked at the rising sun. "I lost my own mother recently too."

The two ladies looked at each other before a high-pitched whistle caught both of their attention. Trinia didn't waste a second before rocketing off at a gallop towards the noise. Not two seconds later, Trakken appeared with Droven on his back, and the two quickly embraced. Droven quickly slipped off Trakken and began walking towards the camp. Windmere and Saralia, with Stephen on her back, soon appeared as well and passed them all at a canter and were shortly in the camp. Stephen slipped off Saralia and walked to his sister.

"Hey, Stephen. How are..." Victoria began before Stephen cut her off by grabbing her in a tight embrace. To her surprise, she saw his eyes were welling up with tears. "What's going on?" she asked as she felt her own eyes begin to water.

"Can we talk? About Mom and Dad, I mean." Stephen sniffed.

"Of course," Victoria replied. She looked at the Trodontians and Droven and told them, "Groman will be waiting for you at his pavilion. We will join you in a little while."

They nodded, and the twins went a little way away into the forest, where they were able talk, cry, and heal from their ordeals.

After the twins had their talk, they rejoined the leaders in the main pavilion, where they were discussing their next move.

"We should try to locate any more artifacts and retrieve them. Any advantage should be used in a situation like this," The Ice Dwarf Frostous said firmly.

"We have been scouring our records and talking with everyone in this camp, and the two artifacts we have now are the only ones we know of," Elder Gilder replied.

"If that is the case, what do we do, now?" Chieftain Galent asked.

"We have those who are chosen to wield them try to unlock their abilities and then figure out a plan from there," Ripper said.

"If I may, I have a theory that may benefit us all if it is true?" Stephen interjected.

"You may proceed, Stephen," Vulant replied.

"When we last encountered Falron, I noticed something during our brief meeting: more like something he didn't do," Stephen said.

"And that is?" The Fire Giant Vesuvian asked.

"His mind control or possession power," Stephen replied. "When we met him the first time, that was his first move. It's a good tactic, really: Divide and conquer. But this time, he used his pyrokinesis to slow us down and then retreated when he felt outmatched."

"What are you getting at?" Peregrine asked.

"Well, Your Majesty, I think Falron has limits to his abilities. He could have easily taken some of us under his control but didn't. Maybe it's because he can't control any more people. And if that's the case with his mind control, it's a reasonable assumption that his other powers have limits too. So maybe we try to find ways to make him use up all his power until he can't anymore?" Stephen replied.

The leaders thought for a moment.

Then, Galent spoke up: "So we are to force him to fight at his maximum potential? Would not attacking a Gritter hive with only a broom be easier?"

"I have the fire covered," Belinda said as she walked into the tent followed by nearly two dozen Flitnao carrying a large trunk. They flew the trunk over to a table, where Belinda opened it and removed a large black helmet with an unusual visor and set it on the table.

Just then, everyone noticed the air around Vesuvian begin to sizzle with heat.

"Is that what I think it is?!" he roared.

"That depends on what you think it is," Belinda replied.

"The cursed firebreak armor worn by Belinda the Traitor who killed my great uncle Krakon during the Blackmian war! I assume that means you are the Belinda of that legend?!" Vesuvian angrily shouted.

"I did not kill him. He took his own life when I offered to spare him," Belinda said quietly.

"If you think I will fight by her side, then you are a fool! I and my tribe will fend for ourselves."

"And fall prey to Falron just like most of the Unkarians and Greatures have?" Groman said firmly. "We need to stand together and face this threat as one."

"Vesuvian, please know I do not take my retrieving this armor lightly. I had buried it on my farm upon my return home many years ago as it was a reminder of how I lost one I had considered a good friend. But now, I see I need to get past that pain and use it one more time to help save this world. I cannot force you to accept my aid, but I can ask," Belinda said. "We need the fierceness and power of the Fire Giants if we are to have any hope of defeating Falron. Will you join us? And if we win, you may do with me and the armor as you please."

Victoria and Annie looked over in surprise at Belinda and Vesuvian visibly cooled down as a grim smile crept across his face.

"You have yourself a deal," he said coldly before walking out of the tent.

Everyone stood in silence, looking at Belinda, who, after a few seconds replaced the helmet in the large trunk and returned to the table. "Now that we've dealt with that, what is our plan?" Belinda asked.

"We should work with those chosen to use the artifacts and learn what they can do or even if they work," Groman suggested.

"I'll help with that," Stephen offered.

"I think that's a great idea, Groman," Victoria said.

"I look forward to seeing the results," Windmere added.

"In the meantime, all soldiers should make ready for battle, and all refugees should prepare to move to a safe location in the event a battle occurs," Elder Gilder said.

"Good thinking," Stephen replied with a nod.

"That settles it, then. We all have tasks to fulfill. We best get to them," Ripper said.

As all the leaders began to filter out of the pavilion, Victoria caught Ripper by the shoulder.

"Do you need something from me?" Ripper asked quietly with a smile.

"I just wanted to say your daughter was amazing on our trip. You've trained her well," Victoria replied, smiling in return.

"She told me everything that happened during your venture," Ripper purred, "including your managing to catch her by surprise. I must say I am impressed with your speed. You have clearly been training in these past two years since we had first met."

With that, Ripper turned and left the pavilion.

Victoria stayed behind in thought. *Speed that can surprise Amronians as skilled as Hannela and Ripper? What is going on with me?* she wondered.

Just then, Stephen poked his head into the tent. "Come on, Tori! Don't you want to find out what the artifacts can do?" he asked before disappearing again.

"I'm right behind you!" Victoria called back as she sprinted to catch up with her brother.

Ten minutes later, Stephen and Victoria had cleared a space under some trees and were joined by Annie, Groman, Droven, Trakken, Trinia, and Saralia.

"Was your aunt going to join us?" Saralia asked.

"She said she had some work to do to get the firebreak armor ready for battle again. She's enlisted your mother's assistance to fix it up," Stephen replied as he surveyed the open space.

"Ah, that would make sense," Trakken said stroking his chin.

"Can Tiny help?" a deep voice came from behind the group.

Stephen, Victoria, and Annie all turned to see their Unkarian friend walking towards them. All three of them ran over to him and hugged him, only to be nearly crushed in his embrace. He quickly released them and took a knee next to the group.

"Tiny sorry to hear about parents. Tiny says Tiny could take care of friends if friends want him to," Tiny said softly.

Tori gave Tiny another hug, and Stephen smiled at him, his eyes watering again.

"Thank you, Tiny. I think we'll be okay, though," Stephen replied quietly.

Tiny nodded and stood up to face the others in the group.

"Alright!" Stephen said loudly after clearing his throat. "Annie, Droven, who wants to go first?"

"Umm..." Annie hesitated.

"Is something wrong, Annie?" Victoria asked.

"Well...I don't know quite how to say this," she replied.

"What is it?" Groman asked.

"It's just that... I don't feel like I can..." Annie replied.

"What do you mean?" Stephen asked.

"It is just that while I can hold it, and I feel like I am the one to use it, I think it needs to be complete before I can wield it," Annie answered.

"Well, that complicates things," Stephen said. "If your feelings are correct, that means we need to get the other half from Falron before we can unlock its power."

"Do we even know what its power was?" Victoria asked.

"The Horiton had mentioned it being able to summon allies at a time of greatest need. Or, at least, that is what the legends say," Groman answered.

"Well maybe since you cannot use it, that means that Falron is unable to as well," Trinia said.

"Let us pray that you are right," Annie said.

"Well, that just leaves you, Droven. Considering what Falron did after taking just a piece of the staff, I think I have a good idea for what it can do," Stephen said.

Droven stepped into the middle of the open area and clasped the staff in his hands tightly. He closed his eyes and took a deep breath, but nothing happened. "I do not know what I am to do," he said sadly.

"Try focusing on a place you want to go. Picture it in your mind," Stephen suggested. "Come to think of it, that may be how Falron appeared where you were, Victoria and Groman."

Droven nodded and closed his eyes again, and this time with a flash of green light, he vanished. Everyone was quickly looking around for him, wondering where he had gone.

"Yes! It works!"

They heard Droven cheering a distance away. They all turned to look only to find him sitting on top of the main pavilion nearly a quarter mile back.

"Now, try to come back to us!" Trakken shouted.

Droven closed his eyes and seemed to concentrate and in a flash of green light was back in the middle of the group once again.

"Well done, soldier!" Groman cheered.

"Thank you, sir!" Droven said with a bow.

"We're not done yet!" Stephen called out as he walked towards Droven. "Now, we should try and see if more than one person can go with him."

"Can I try?" Victoria asked.

"Absolutely," Droven replied.

Stephen and Victoria put their hands on Droven's shoulders and looked at him.

"Where to, sir?" Droven asked with a grin.

"Well, how about Prariat?" Stephen suggested. "That's a good distance away."

"As you wish!" Droven said excitedly.

"Wait! No!" Saralia cried as she rushed towards them, but it was too late. In a flash of green light, the trio were gone.

To the three travelers it seemed like they were walking through a tunnel made of green lights, and only seconds later, they appeared in a ruined city.

"Here we are!" Droven said loudly.

"Wait. Where is everybody?" Victoria said in a hushed tone.

"I thought Prariat was still standing," Stephen said quietly.

"They had been under siege for weeks. Groman and our troops were able to break it long enough to the citizens to escape. Falron left shortly afterwards as there was nobody left to control," Droven said in a whisper.

"Did I?" A familiar voice called out from a nearby house.

"Droven, take us back! Now!" Stephen said in a panic.

"Oh, thank you for bringing that to me!" Falron said as he appeared in the doorway. Stephen noticed his half of the horn was hanging from his belt.

"Anytime, Droven!" Victoria hissed.

"I am trying!" Droven said as he clenched his eyes shut.

Suddenly, the green tunnel appeared again, and in moments, the three were back at the camp with their friends. Their sudden appearance caused the Trodontians to rear up in surprise. Stephen and Victoria quickly let go of Droven and sat down in the grass.

"Well, that was cutting it too close," Stephen said panting.

"What happened?" Trakken asked.

"We went to Prariat, alright. And Falron was there," Victoria replied.

"I was about to tell you before you vanished. Falron likely took the city after everyone left. Groman's forces gave us just enough time to evacuate the city," Saralia said with her hands on her sides.

"Well, now we know we can take multiple people in one jump," Stephen said as he got to his feet. "Shall we try again? Maybe with more people this time?"

"Are you sure that is wise?" Droven hesitated.

"Do you feel alright, Droven?" Annie asked.

"I am alright. The times I traveled with someone else felt like my strength was draining a little. More people may take more energy from me."

"Let's just try jumping to another place and back again. Then, you can take a break?" Stephen suggested.

"Alright," Droven said as he held the staff in front of him again. Stephen and Victoria put their hands on his shoulders again.

"I'm coming this time," Annie said as she grabbed Victoria's free hand.

"I shall join you as well," Groman said as he took Stephen's free hand. "If that is alright with you, Droven?"

"I will be fine." Droven replied. "Where shall we go this time?"

"Somewhere safe and far from Falron," Victoria said.

"Alright." Droven held the staff tightly and concentrated. To everyone's horror, the staff seemed to crack as the green light began to envelop them.

"What was that?" Stephen said as they were transported away from their friends.

Just as suddenly as it came the light vanished and the five of them were in a large room with a raised platform on one side and pews on the other.

"I'm not sure what happened. But it looks like we are in some sort of church...on Earth!" Victoria said in shock.

Droven started breathing heavily and sat down in the front row.

"Droven!" Groman gasped.

"I will be alright. I just need to catch my breath," Droven said, panting.

"I guess it really does take it out of him," Victoria mused as she looked around the room. It was the auditorium of an old church, alright. The whole place smelled like many old buildings she had been in. There was a balcony across from the platform where the pulpit was. A large wooden backdrop was behind the pulpit, and fake plants were scattered around the stage. There was a large window above them to the right of the stage that was covered with a curtain.

"Well, since we are on Earth, I don't think we're in any danger. Take your time to rest, Droven," Stephen said as he walked up to the pulpit. "Maybe the staff cracked as we were pushing you too hard."

"I do not think that was the cause," Droven said. "It felt like the staff was taking everyone's ideas of where to go and it was overwhelmed."

"Well, that's good to know for next time," Annie said.

"Be silent!" Groman suddenly hissed. "Someone is coming!"

The group all froze as they heard someone talking while getting closer to where they were.

Just then, the double doors to their right opened up, and a young man who looked to be in his late twenties walked in while talking on a phone. He was average height but on the stockier side with short brown hair that was speckled with grey and a large pair of glasses. He was wearing a red T-shirt and blue jeans, but to everyone's surprise he wore a hand-and-a-half sword on his belt.

"Yes, Jeremy, I'll be there soon, depending on how bad the traffic is, anyways. Look, you all can wait for me at the gate, or you can go on in and look around while I drive to the faire," he said before noticing the five adventurers. His eyes widened in shock. "Uh, something just came up. I may be a little later than I expected. I'll see you soon." He slowly lowered the smartphone and looked at the group. Annie, Groman, and Droven said nothing but vanished. At this, the man pocketed the phone and held his hand over his sword. "Who are you, and where did you come from? Where did your friends go? Why did they not look human? How did you get in here?" The man asked questions rapidly.

Stephen held up his hands and slowly approached the man. "Calm down. We don't mean any harm. We just stopped by for a rest; that's all."

"Considering this building is locked up tight at all times, I highly doubt you came in the normal way," the man responded. "Did you teleport in here or something?"

"In short, yes. Look, we aren't here to cause trouble. Just go on your way to wherever you were going, and we'll be out of your hair quickly enough," Victoria said.

"I'm the live-in security guard here in this church. It's my job to deal with people who break in. You're lucky I was on my way to renaissance faire, or I'd have something a bit more powerful on hand," the man said as he stepped closer to Stephen.

"That sounds like a fun afternoon," Stephen replied calmly. "I've spent many days at the faires near my home. I even got trained in sword fighting with a group there. I'm sorry we interrupted your plans."

"I'd say I'm used to crazy stuff happening, being that I used to work retail, but this is something completely different," the man said as he relaxed his posture. "So are you going to tell me what, or who, you are?"

"I'm Stephen, and this is my sister Victoria," Stephen replied.

"What about your other friends?"

At this question, Groman, Annie, and Droven reappeared near the twins.

"I am Groman, this is my sister Annalio and our friend Droven. We are of the Kittrian tribe of Lulandal," Groman replied.

"So you're not elves?" the man asked.

"Nope!" Annie said with a little laugh.

"What are elves?" Droven asked, looking completely confused.

"I'll explain later," Stephen replied.

"So let me get this straight: You five just teleported here from another world?" the man asked.

"Pretty much, yes." Victoria answered.

"I assume you can go back to this world? Not that I'm kicking you out; you all seem decent enough, and I get the feeling if you wanted to cause trouble, you would have already," the man said as he sat in a front row pew.

"We will return once our friend Droven is rested and ready to take us there," Groman said as he looked over to Droven who at this point had laid down on a pew.

"Give me ten minutes, and I will be ready to try again," Droven said as he closed his eyes.

"That gives me more time to ask you some questions," the man said.

"Depending on what they are, I'm not sure we should answer them," Stephen said.

"I can understand your hesitation," the man replied. "I can only imagine what would happen if the our world knew about another world, with untold possibilities just out of their reach. You have my word as an author that I will not reveal your secret."

"You're an author?" Victoria asked.

"Well..." The Author started as his face turned as red as his shirt. "I'd like to be one someday; I just can't work out a good story."

"We could tell you ours!" Annie suggested.

"We do not have the time right now. Falron may follow us here," Groman interjected.

"Falron? Who's that?" The Author asked.

"An evil man from this world who is out to conquer their world and probably ours once he gets enough power," Stephen answered.

"So you're just trying to beat a bad guy?" The Author questioned.

"In short, yes," Groman said.

"But he has proven to be incredibly powerful," Droven added.

"He'll be a tough one to beat, that's for sure," Stephen finished.

"I have an idea that might help you," The Author said before pointing at Stephen. "You're over eighteen, right?"

"By a few months, yes," Stephen answered. "Why?"

The Author said nothing but disappeared through a set of double doors and beckoned Stephen to follow, which he did. The two men went up a flight of stairs into a small apartment on the upper story. Stephen looked around at the stacks of books lying around as well as an array of swords in one corner. He gingerly picked one up that had a familiar blue and gold sheath with a golden triangle emblem and partially pulled the blade out.

"That's just a prop weapon," The Author said as he entered the bedroom, "Most of those are. I do have a few real swords but nothing that would be of more use than this." The Author reached behind the bedroom door and pulled out a large case. He set it on the bed and then pulled out an old ammo box and set it down next to the case. Taking a key from the carabiner on his belt loop, the man unlocked the case, opened it, then stepped aside.

Stephen looked at what was inside and felt his jaw drop. "Is that...?" he began.

"Model eighteen ninety-seven trench gun. She's built for close quarters combat; the slam-fire function still works, which is perfect for laying down covering fire or clearing a group of enemies, and I've got the bayonet for her too," the man replied with a grin as he handed Stephen a large knife in a sheath.

"Look, you're not coming with us, no matter what you say," Stephen said, turning to face the man.

"I know that. I'm letting you take this and the bandolier of ammo I've got for it. That should be enough firepower to deal with whatever bad guy you run into. I'd like to see some sort of evil wizard try to tank double-odd buckshot."

"I can't take this," Stephen said.

"Yes, you can. Look, I'm just a guy who likes to try and help people however possible. It's logical that you're telling the truth about what and who you are. Maybe by giving you this, I can persuade you to return here to the Midwest and tell me more about this world; maybe not. But whatever the case, you have friends and family to protect over there; I'm sure of that. So take it and win that fight!" The Author replied.

Stephen looked longingly at the weapon and held out his hand for the author to shake.

"I'm beginning to think that God brought us here for a pretty good reason," Stephen said as he strapped the shotgun to his back and threw the bandolier over his shoulder.

"He can work however He wants. It's up to us to give Him the glory no matter what happens afterwards. Speaking of which, I really need to get going. My brother, his wife, and his daughter are waiting for me."

"Have fun! I hope you can learn some good sword fighting skills while you're there," Stephen said with a laugh as he left the room.

He soon walked downstairs and saw his friends were waiting for him.

"Stephen, what were you doing up there?" Annie asked.

"Just making a deal with that guy," Stephen replied.

Groman took hold of Droven's shoulder. "We need to return to our friends in my world. Are you ready, Droven?"

"Yes," Droven replied.

As the twins walked over to Droven, Victoria stared at Stephen's acquisition.

"Is that a shotgun?" she asked in bewilderment.

"It is, indeed. The Author said I can have it as long as I track him down after we win and tell him more about us. He probably wants to write a story about our adventures."

"How exciting!" Annie said as everyone held hands, and the green light covered them again. Stephen caught a glimpse of The Author watching them from his window before they were taken away and brought back to Lulandal.

When they arrived, they found everyone was still right where they had left them. Trakken and Trinia were holding hands, while Tiny and Saralia were arm wrestling nearby. Just as they appeared, Tiny smacked Saralia's arm down on the table and jumped to his feet in victory before seeing his friends return.

"Friends home!" Tiny shouted.

Droven took a step back and fell to his knees gasping for air. "That last one really took my energy away. Can we do another test tomorrow?" he asked.

"Sure thing, Droven," Stephen said, helping him to his feet. "You've done more than enough for today."

Trakken, Trinia, and Tiny all walked over to the group just as Droven froze in fear.

"Falron is coming! I can feel the power he took from it nearby!" Droven said in horror.

"Just like how I can sense the source's whereabouts," Falron's voice came from above them.

Stephen quickly cupped his hands over his mouth and shouted: "Evacuate the camp now! We'll keep him busy!" Stephen pulled the shotgun out and started loading shells into the magazine.

"Stay behind me, my love!" Trakken said as he quickly moved in front of Trinia, who hid behind his large body.

Just then, a figure cloaked in black dropped down from a tree a short distance away. His hood fell back to reveal Falron's gaunt face grinning like a madman.

"Stephen, Victoria, take hold of our friends. I will get us away from here and hopefully lead Falron away," Droven whispered.

The twins didn't question him but quietly touched their friends, and suddenly, the green light began to cover them again.

"No!!!" Falron shouted as he let lose a blast of flames towards them. But it was too late as the light took them somewhere else.

Within seconds, they were all left in a wide-open grassy plain with rolling hills and a few lone trees dotted about.

"Where are we?" Groman asked in surprise.

"It reminds me of the Shadowed Prairie, but there are more hills and fewer trees," Saralia commented.

Suddenly, Droven groaned and fell down with a thud. Groman quickly checked him and looked up at his friends.

"He is unconscious but well. I would say he will be resting for a while," Groman said.

"What do we do, now?" Trinia asked.

"We should look around and see where we are," Saralia suggested.

"Finding shelter would be a good idea too," Victoria added. "I don't want to leave Droven just lying around here in the open. What if Falron also tracks us here?"

Everyone nodded, and together, they started climbing the nearest hill, with Tiny carrying Droven. At the top, they saw a large stream flowing though the plains, and a little way past that, they spotted an old roadway with a tiny gas station set on it facing away from them.

"Everyone, get down," Stephen hissed.

They all hid behind the hilltop and looked at Stephen.

"What did you see?" Trakken asked.

"A gas station," Stephen replied.

"And that is?" Saralia asked.

"Precisely. We're on Earth," Stephen replied.

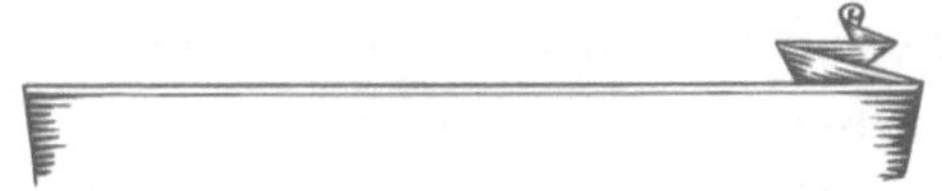

# Chapter 8. What it takes.

"You mean to say we are in your world?!" Trinia asked in surprise.

"Yes, and the less this world knows of you, the better. I don't want to think about what would happen if they learned you existed," Stephen said.

"So now what do we do?" Annie asked.

"I'm going to that station and see if anyone saw us. If so, I'll try to find a way to keep the news from leaking out," Stephen replied. *Good thing I didn't change out of my Earth clothes. It should be no problem for Victoria and me to walk in and out*, he thought.

"I'll go too," Victoria said as she took the thick leather shirt she was wearing off and removed her weaponry.

"Me too," Annie said.

"I'm sorry, Annie, but you don't look human enough to go unnoticed by our world," Stephen said as he left his weapons in the tall grass.

Annie huffed as she pulled out a pair of sunglasses from a pocket and put them on while her skin color turned from an earthy brown to a more human tone and her long white hair turned blonde. She then used her hair to cover her long ears and put her hands in her pockets.

"How's this?" Annie asked.

"I assume you have done this before?" Groman asked.

"Belinda may have snuck me into town a few times, so I could experience Earth while I was staying with her," Annie said with a giggle.

"I guess you can come along," Stephen said with a smile. "The rest of you should stay out of sight until we return."

Soon, Stephen, Victoria, and Annie were making their way across the shallow stream, using a fallen tree as a bridge. When they got to the station, Stephen checked the back for cameras. Finding none, they went around to the front of the building and saw it was a modest establishment. There were only four pumps under an aging canopy and a single rusty pickup truck parked off to the side; the windows were clean, and an "Open" sign was hanging from the door.

"Shall we go in?" Stephen asked.

Victoria and Annie nodded, and together, they opened the door, causing a little bell to ring. The store seemed old but well taken care of. Everything was cleaned and well stocked; the smell of fresh coffee and donuts greeted them as they entered the building.

"Hello!" a voice called out from the back of the store. A middle-aged woman with long fiery red hair wearing a blue uniform appeared from a back room. "I'm sorry, I didn't hear you pull up. Is there something I can get for you?"

"No, thanks, we're just browsing," Victoria said with a smile. She noticed Annie snooping around the candy aisle.

"Do you happen to have any gummy worms?" Annie asked.

"Why, of course, sweetie," the worker said as she hurried over. "We have several different brands and both sweet and sour worms."

"Thanks!" Annie said as she selected a bag.

"What's up with your hand?" the worker asked.

"Oh, uh, I was born this way?" Annie said as she quickly dropped the bag and hid her hands in her pockets.

"I'm sorry, I didn't mean to offend you," the worker said.

"Excuse me? Can I ask you a question?" Stephen called out from another side of the store.

"Of course!" the worker quickly replied as she walked over.

"Okay, so I may sound dumb, but I wasn't really paying attention to the map while we were driving. Where are we?"

"You're not dumb at all, sweetie, you're in western Nebraska. Or, as I like to call it, the middle of nowhere," the worker said with a sigh. "Nothing ever happens 'round these parts; only reason this place is still around is Daddy wanted to keep it running despite our other stores near the interstate being much busier. But this one was the first, so I guess he's sentimental about it. I wish someday a tornado would just come through and take this place with it, so I can finally work at the good stores."

"Uh, thanks," Stephen said hesitantly.

Suddenly, they heard a knock at the window. Everyone turned to see what it was, and to the shock of Stephen, Victoria and Annie, it was Trinia. She had come close to the door where her lower half was still hidden below the window.

"Is that another friend of yours?" the worker asked the trio before turning to the window. "Come on in, sweetheart! The door's unlocked!"

Trinia quickly shook her head no before a loud honking made her rear up on her hind legs in surprise. The worker gasped in shock and raced outside, followed by Stephen, Victoria, and Annie. There, the worker looked to her left and saw Trinia frozen in fear before turning to her right and seeing the massive form of Tiny walking towards her. Tiny got within a few feet of the worker before smiling, showing her his rows of sharp teeth.

The worker promptly fainted.

"Tiny sorry. Tiny was trying to be quiet, but Tiny bump strange metal box, and metal box made loud noise," Tiny said sheepishly.

"Well, now, we're really in a fix," Stephen said as he found the keys to the truck on the worker's belt and shut off the alarm.

"What are you doing here, Trinia?" Victoria asked.

"Groman sent me to retrieve you. Droven started talking in his sleep. He says Falron is searching for the staff again," Trinia replied. "Tiny was to stay nearby if you had been detained for some reason."

"What about Trakken and Saralia?" Annie asked.

"They are scouting for better shelter," Trinia replied.

"Tiny not think there will be better place than this," Tiny said with a grunt. He looked at the metal bollards that lined the front of the store. Turning to Stephen, he asked, "Strange trees make good club?"

"I guess, though they would be hard to..." Stephen began but was cut off by Tiny taking one with both hands and ripping it from the concrete. He held it in his hands and looked at the concrete that was still clinging to the bottom.

"Tiny like these strange trees," Tiny said with a smile before shouldering it and walking away.

"What are we going to do, now?" Victoria asked. "She's going to come to any minute."

"I'll put her in her truck and drive her away from here. Maybe I'll come up with an explanation for what she's seen before then. Meanwhile, you three go back to Groman and see if we can come up a plan for if or when Falron finds us," Stephen said as he began to drag the worker over towards the pickup.

"It's better than nothing," Victoria said with a sigh.

Trinia shuddered and pawed nervously at the loose gravel beneath her white hooves. "Do you think he can find us?"

"It's hard to guess," Annie said as they began walking back towards where they had left Groman and Droven.

After about half an hour, Stephen returned on foot to find everyone waiting for him.

"Did you manage to convince her she didn't just see what she thought she saw wandering around?" Victoria asked.

"I don't know," Stephen said. "She came to when I parked the truck, and I told her she had passed out after hallucinating. I said it was probably a gas leak or something and that she needs to stay away from that station to let the gas go away. When I told her I used the keys on her belt to lock up the station, she didn't argue but thanked me for helping her and drove away."

"Well, let's hope she doesn't return with a massive news crew or the army," Victoria replied.

"So what is our plan now?" Trakken asked.

"Droven is still resting; I would estimate he will still be resting for a few hours more," Groman said.

"But we may not have hours if Falron is looking for us," Trinia said as she edged closer to Trakken, who put his arm around her.

"I have an idea, but it's a risky one," Victoria said.

"Risky may be our only option," Saralia replied. "Go on."

"We use that station as a trap and somehow lure Falron into it," Victoria suggested.

"Are you saying we should blow up the station?" Stephen asked.

"It may be our best opportunity to take Falron down. There's probably enough fuel under it to send him into oblivion. All we have to do is figure out a way to lure him in somehow and then light the gas," Victoria replied.

"I agree with Victoria," Groman said. "If that is our best hope, then I say we take it."

"Hear, hear!" Trakken added.

"How about someone carves another staff like the Wanderer's Staff, and we use it as bait?" Saralia asked.

"Good thinking," Stephen said.

"I do like carving in my spare time," Trinia added.

"Perfect!" Annie said excitedly.

"I will need time to find the right staff and carve it like the original."

"And we will need time to prepare the station for detonation," Stephen added. "Trakken and Trinia can handle making the bait. Tiny, Annie, Saralia, and I can handle preparing the trap. Victoria, you and Groman can keep watch over Droven. Let us know if he says anything else."

"Right," Victoria said as her face turned a little red.

Trakken and Trinia quickly galloped away to find a suitable piece of wood, while the others went back to the station. There, at the direction of Stephen, they began to rig the pumps so that fuel was leaking everywhere.

"Water smell strange," Tiny said as he brought a handful to his nose.

"Don't drink it!" Stephen said quickly. "That stuff is not good for you."

Tiny nodded and let the gas out of his massive hands.

"Annie, can you go inside and see if you can find some gas cans?" Stephen asked as he watched Tiny smash the last pump.

"Sure!" Annie replied quickly before running inside. She returned within minutes with two small gallon cans, and Stephen noticed her pockets were full of gummy worm bags. He rolled his eyes but said nothing.

Stephen filled the two cans with fuel and began pouring it out in a trail leading away from the station. As he walked, he called out to Saralia. "Can you make some fire arrows? We'll need them to ignite this place once Falron takes the bait."

"If I can find the right materials," Saralia said as she quickly galloped away.

"Alright, we need to leave this place, now!" Stephen shouted to Annie and Tiny. "If you can, wash off that stuff in the stream. I don't want anyone other than Falron catching fire."

Tiny and Annie made their way to the stream, and Trakken galloped over and showed off the fake staff. It looked just like the original.

"Perfect!" Stephen exclaimed. "Just set it in the middle of those pumps. Maybe Falron will be so overcome with his lust for the power, he won't realize he's in a trap."

"We can certainly hope," Trakken said as he hurried away.

Soon, the trap was set, and everyone was in place. The fake staff was sitting on a pile of some fertilizer bags Stephen had found. Everyone else was on a hill overlooking the trap with a small fire going. Saralia had managed to make three fire arrows, and the heads of which were sitting in the flames, so they were ready to go. Trinia kept to the back, watching over Droven, who was still sleeping. Groman paced nearby, with Annie quietly sitting near the fire, snacking on the gummy worms. Stephen, Victoria, Saralia, and Trakken had cleaned up their weapons and were prepared for a fight.

Just as the sun was beginning to sink lower in the late afternoon sky, Stephen spotted a flash of green light between them and the station.

"He's here!" he hissed. Saralia quickly took up her bow and laid a flaming arrow on the string.

"Remember where the target is; once you hit that, the whole place should go up in flames," Victoria whispered, pointing out the small spot they had marked in the grass.

Stephen watched as Falron looked around and saw the fake staff. He seemed to laugh and then slowly walked over to the trap.

"He's taking the bait!" he said excitedly. Just then, to his horror, Falron seemed to look right at where they were hiding. He saw Falron's hands raise and then nearly four dozen shadow warriors appeared and rushed towards their position.

"Incoming!" Victoria called out.

"He's there! Saralia, light him up!" Stephen yelled as he racked the slide on the shotgun, chambering a shell.

Saralia took aim and loosed the arrow. To everyone's horror, one of the shadows jumped in front of it and took the arrow to the chest, causing it to disintegrate.

"Keep trying!" Stephen yelled. "This is going to get noisy!" He pulled the trigger, and the shotgun let out a blast of buckshot, causing several shadows to vanish before they reached their ranks. Saralia readied another arrow and fired, it, too, being caught by a shadow.

"No!" Saralia screamed as she grabbed the last one from the fire pit.

Stephen started firing as fast as he could reload the trench gun. The shadows were nearly upon them, now.

"Gather around Droven and Trinia! Let nothing pass you!" Groman shouted as he readied his large weapon.

Saralia readied the last arrow, and just as she released the bowstring, a shadow threw a rock, which hit her hand, causing her arrow to fly harmlessly into the stream below them. Saralia drew her scimitars and quickly began fighting the shadows.

"I will set off the trap! Take care of my Trinia!" Trakken roared as he thundered away at full gallop smashing through the shadows and racing down the hill.

"Trakken!" Trinia screamed after him.

Trakken crossed the stream without slowing down and was soon at the place that Stephen had marked. He was about use his flint and steel when he heard a voice from in front of him.

"Nice trap. Too bad you'll be the one to get caught in it," Falron said with a laugh as rounded the opposite side of the station. His eyes turned from violet to red as he let loose a burst of flames towards the trap. His eyes then turned green, and he vanished away.

The heroes on the hill saw most of it, Falron confronting Trakken, his shooting fire and then vanishing, which also caused the shadows to fade away. But what nobody could miss was the massive fireball that erupted from the station, lighting up the whole area like it was high noon and the flaming limp body of Trakken getting blown into the stream.

Trinia's scream echoed through Stephen's ears as she fell to the ground sobbing. Tiny and Saralia rushed towards the stream.

"Is he...?!" Annie asked in shock.

"Dead?" Stephen replied. "I don't know."

# Chapter 9. To be a true hero.

Stephen quickly ran down the hill with Groman to see if Trakken was alright. Saralia had laid down next to his burned body and was busy spreading an orange paste on the wounds.

"Is he alive?" Groman asked.

"Yes, but barely," Saralia answered without looking up from her work.

Tiny was rubbing his hands together and getting ready to heal Trakken.

"Tiny, stop!" Stephen panted. "If you try to heal him now, you'll be unconscious for the rest of the day. We need you awake right now. Can you carry him once Saralia says it's safe to?"

Tiny stopped, and his expression turned to one of sorrow and understanding. Saralia got up on her four legs and looked at Tiny and nodded. Tiny very gently picked up Trakken, and the four of them made their way up the hill. It was then Stephen noticed the true extent of the damage: Trakken's hindquarters were very badly burned, and his hind legs seemed twisted and broken.

"Do you think Tiny can even heal that kind of damage?" Stephen whispered to Groman.

"I do not know," Groman replied sorrowfully, "but you are right. We need him awake if Falron comes back for us."

When they rejoined the others, Trinia slowly came over to Trakken and clasped his big hands in hers. To Stephen's surprise, Droven was on his feet, albeit unsteadily.

"I must get you all away from here," Droven said firmly.

Nobody argued, but they all took each other's hands, and the green light appeared and whisked them away.

When it retreated, they found themselves in a large clearing between an oceanside cliff and a thick forest. Stephen looked around at the clearing and spotted a few rock outcroppings around them with sparse vegetation. Far off in the distance, he spotted what he guessed was a small fishing boat silhouetted by the setting sun.

"We're home," Annie said, relieved.

"Yes, you are, little one!" a voice called out.

Stephen's heart sank, as he knew who it was. He looked over and saw Falron appearing near to the cliff edge, a wicked grin on his face. "Falron," he said coldly, "you're going to pay for all the pain you've caused."

"Tiny, get my brother and Trinia out of here, now," Saralia said as she laid an arrow on the string. "I do not want my future sister-in-law to see what I am about to do to this monster."

Tiny did not argue and took off at a sprint, with Trinia galloping after him.

Stephen loaded up the shotgun again and prepared to give it everything he had. Everyone drew their weapons, and even Droven, who was swaying on his feet, held his sword at the ready.

Falron laughed, and his eyes turned violet.

"Prepare for shadows!" Stephen shouted as he racked the shotgun once again and fixed the bayonet to the barrel.

The shadows appeared between Falron and the heroes, rows upon rows of them, and to Stephen's horror, the first two lines were made up entirely of archers.

"Take cover!" Victoria screamed as everyone tried to find some protection.

The shadow archers loosed their arrows, and Stephen heard their whistling through the air as he ran. He looked back and saw them coming down like mosquitoes, thwacking into the ground.

He suddenly saw Droven fall behind the group with two arrows in his back. Droven sank to his knees as the shadows began to run towards them. But it was what he heard next that made Stephen stop running: It was his sister screaming.

"I'm hit!" Victoria shrieked.

Stephen turned around and saw Victoria limping towards Groman, who was quickly running back to her. An arrow was in her right leg.

"No...NO!" Stephen heard himself roar. He sprinted towards Victoria and Groman. "Groman, get her out of here, now!" he shouted as he fired his shotgun into the oncoming mass of shadow warriors.

"But what about Droven?" Victoria asked through her tears.

"I'll get him, now, go!" Stephen repeated. He spotted the black cloak of Falron approaching Droven, who was back on his feet and in the same fighting stance he had taught him all those years ago.

"I will come with you," Groman said.

"No."

"But—"

"Excalibur!" Stephen shouted as he rushed into the fray, spraying buckshot into any shadows that came too close.

Groman's body went white as a sheet as he picked up Victoria and began to run towards Saralia.

"What are you doing?! Put me down! I can make it to Saralia!" Victoria shouted in his ear.

Groman said nothing to her but kept up his pace. He then shouted, "Saralia! I am ordering you to take Victoria to the healing tent and then send help! The camp should only be a short distance from here."

Saralia nodded and took Victoria from him.

"Let me go and help you!" Victoria pleaded.

"You are not in any shape to fight," Groman said firmly. "I will go back for him." He turned to Annie, who had just run up, an arrow sticking out of her left prosthetic leg. "Go with them."

Annie nodded and climbed onto Saralia's back, and Saralia took off at a gallop towards where the camp was.

Groman drew the Empty Sword from his back and looked at where Stephen was fighting his way through the shadows. "You may have invoked the vow, that does not mean I am not going to try and rescue you too," he said to himself before running back towards the battle.

As soon as Groman carried Victoria away, Stephen rushed towards the shadows. The archers let loose another volley, but he dodged the arrows and started pumping their ranks full of buckshot. Each shell would make several shadows disappear, but there seemed to be so many. He cleared the ranks of archers and charged towards the warriors, who had their weapons drawn. He slung the trench gun over his shoulder and drew his sword, cutting his way through them. He soon saw Droven, surrounded by warriors, bleeding from many wounds on top of the two arrows in his back but somehow still standing.

Droven turned to see Stephen approaching and managed a weak smile. "I held them as long as I could," he gasped.

Stephen stepped forward, only for four shadow knights in full plate armor and wielding spears to appear between them. The first one swung its spear, and Stephen countered by catching the spear between his arm and body and wrenching it away from the knight. He quickly switched to his shotgun again; he racked the slide and blasted the shadow knight away. The next knight came at him, and Stephen managed to block the attack with the shotgun. He pushed the knight away, buying himself time to reload five more shells into the magazine. He quickly blasted through the last three knights, only to be greeted by the sight of Droven facing him on his knees with Falron behind him.

"I did my duty for Lulandal!" Droven managed with his last breath as Falron slid his sword into Droven's back.

The lifeless body of Droven fell to the ground as Falron picked up the staff. Stephen watched as the staff turned grey, disintegrated into dust, and blew away in the sea breeze.

"Ah, now that's the stuff I was looking for!" Falron said happily.

"Why are you doing this?!" Stephen shouted as he felt two warriors grab his arms from behind. "Why take over this world?!"

"Why not?!" Falron said with a laugh. "This world has incredible powers that one can use to not only rule it, but others as well."

"If you're so powerful, then why don't you fight me one on one?!" Stephen spat at him.

Falron looked at him with feigned shock. "Why not, indeed? I could use a workout," Falron said as he threw off his cloak, revealing his gaunt shirtless torso and black and white striped pants. With a snap of his fingers, Falron's shadows disappeared, freeing Stephen from their clutches.

"Stephen!" Groman shouted from behind Stephen.

"Oh, no, no, no! Interrupting is rude, don't you know?!" Falron shouted back. His eyes changed from violet to red.

"Groman, look out!" Stephen called back as Falron let loose a blast of fire, making a wall and cutting Groman off from the two combatants. The wall of fire grew to about ten feet tall and changed color from red to blue. Groman gasped and fell to his knees as the heat drained his energy.

"There. Now, we won't be bothered," Falron said as he looked at Stephen.

Stephen closed his eyes and took a deep breath. He heard Falron scream and looked up to see him rushing towards him with his fists ablaze in the same blue fire. Stephen jumped back and fired his shotgun. Falron teleported a foot to his left, dodging the shot. He then threw a fireball at Stephen, who ducked down and fired another shot, which Falron dodged.

"You really have to try harder than that," Falron laughed as he appeared behind Stephen.

Stephen swung around and tried to slash Falron with the bayonet but missed him by a hair. Falron swung in with another fiery punch, which Stephen blocked with the shotgun. Falron jumped back and let loose with another long blast of fire, causing Stephen to sprint out of its range. Stephen quickly jumped backwards and fired off another shot, this one also being dodged by Falron, who nimbly teleported away.

"Two shots left, kid!" Falron taunted. "Better get in close for the kill!" He sprinted towards Stephen with his sword drawn.

Stephen fired another shot, but, once again, Falron dodged by teleporting even closer to Stephen, grabbing the shotgun and wrenching it from him, throwing it aside.

Stephen drew his sword and rushed towards Falron, who drew his own sword, and they locked blades.

"My parents told me I was to be the ruler of a new world order, and with this power, I can finally achieve that goal!" Falron laughed.

"My parents told me I was to protect my world and my family. I've already accomplished that. How about you?" Stephen said grimly.

Falron growled and pushed Stephen back before launching into a series of repeated sword strikes, hacking away at Stephen's defenses.

"You will lose! It is inevitable!" Falron shouted with each swing.

Stephen desperately kept blocking the attacks, but after one particularly hard strike, he saw a crack begin to form on his blade. Before he had time to switch to his dagger, Falron hit his weapon again and this time shattered his sword.

"Now, you die!" Falron screamed as he lunged at Stephen, who drew his dagger and managed to deflect the blow. "Still have some fight left in you, eh? Just like your friend who had the staff, oh, what was his name?"

Falron teleported behind Stephen and lunged again. But this time, Stephen stepped to the side and caught the blade between his arm and torso. Turning, he disarmed Falron, pulling the weapon away and tossing the blade over the cliff. Falron looked at Stephen with disbelief before teleporting away again, and Stephen quickly found him to his left. Gripping his dagger, Stephen rushed towards Falron.

"His name was Droven. And he will be the last person you will kill!"

Falron gasped as he felt Stephen drive the dagger deep into his stomach. He struggled to take in his next breath, yet his eyes had an evil, victorious look to them as he looked down at the hero. "Oh...really?"

Stephen felt an icy sensation come over him and looked down. Falron had picked up Stephen's broken sword hilt. The same hilt that was now buried in his chest. The two combatants separated and staggered backwards. Stephen felt weaker by the second as he noticed a purple light coming from Falron's wound with the dagger still inside him.

"What have you done?" Falron screamed. "I can't...I can't contain the power!"

Suddenly a blast of purple energy erupted from Falron's wound, knocking Stephen back against a large boulder. Falron was down on the ground at the edge of the fire wall. Stephen felt his life slipping from him as he noticed Groman was crawling towards him from the other side of the wall. He felt another icy feeling coming from his left arm and saw his own dagger was firmly embedded into it, having been blown into him by the blast of energy. Just when he thought it couldn't get any worse, he felt the ground begin give way under him as the cliff face started to crumble.

"St...Stephen..." Groman gasped.

"Groman...listen...to me closely," Stephen said weakly. "When Monaria said one of us...was going to die...I had a feeling it was going to be me. That's why I want...you to swear that you...will take care of my sister...for me. Her safety...means everything to me."

"I will," Groman said. "You have my word."

"Good," Stephen said as he coughed up some blood. "I know...she means a lot...to you, too, and you to her. Now, catch."

Stephen tossed a small black object over the wall of flames, and it landed in the grass by Groman. Groman took it and saw it was the other half of the Horn of the Horiton.

"I cut it off his belt. Make sure...to use that wisely," Stephen said as he saw Falron rise to his feet, his eyes glowing red and brighter than they had before. Stephen looked to his right and noticed the shotgun with one more shell in the chamber lying nearby. "Promise me...you're going to finish off this lunatic," he said to Groman, who was trying to get to his feet.

"Yes, we will take him together," Groman replied.

Stephen coughed. "Yeah, you and Tori will." He laughed again and quickly rolled over to grab the shotgun. Using his right arm, he aimed it at Falron, the madman's expression turning from anger to shock and fear.

"Goodbye, Groman," Stephen said as he pulled the trigger.

The recoil sent the shotgun flying past Stephen and off the cliff into the waters below. The buckshot caught Falron off guard, as he didn't have time to dodge it. Instead, the blast blew off part of Falron's left arm. Shrieking in pain, Falron gripped the bloody stump, and Groman watched in horror as the purple energy erupted out of the wound and blasted the ground in front of Stephen like a cannon.

The wall of fire disappeared, and Groman felt his strength returning slowly. But as he got to his feet, the ground shook, as a large chunk of the cliff, with Stephen's unconscious body lying on it, fell away into the ocean below.

Stephen didn't feel any pain as he fell. He looked down to see the water hundreds of feet below filled with rocks and debris.

He closed his eyes and thought, *I did what I could. It's up to you now, Groman and Victoria. Go save the world.*

Then, everything went white, and he felt no more.

"No!" Groman screamed as he watched his friend—his brother—fall into the water. He heard a shriek above him and saw the grey and black form of Peregrine diving towards the waters in the hopes she would catch him.

"No, you don't!" Falron shouted, and a torrent of flames shot out of his right hand like a blanket over the area, forcing Peregrine to pull out of the dive to keep from getting roasted.

Suddenly, more Blackmians and Horiton swarmed the area, with Vulant rushing to Groman's side.

"I will take you to the camp," Vulant said quickly as he grabbed Groman and took off.

"What about Falron?" Groman asked.

"He just vanished, sir!" one of the Horiton called back.

"Probably to lick his wounds in peace," Vulant replied.

"Search the rocks at the shoreline! You must find Stephen!" Groman shouted.

The warriors nodded and dove for the shore, with Peregrine taking point. Vulant flew Groman back to the camp in silence, for neither knew what to say.

When the tops of the tents came into view, Groman finally spoke up. "Take me to the healing tents. I...I must tell Victoria the news," he said quietly.

Vulant nodded and quickly dove down and dropped Groman off outside before taking off again.

Groman was about to reach for the tent flap when he heard something land behind him.

"Groman..." Peregrine's voice quivered behind him.

Groman turned around and saw Peregrine, dripping with seawater and her eyes full of tears, holding a bloody shirt, some scraps of metal, and wood that looked like they came from Stephen's strange weapon.

"This...this is all we found...everything else is buried under rubble and water. I am...I am so...so sorry..." Peregrine said through tears.

Groman took the bloody shirt and scraps of metal and felt his own eyes begin to sting with hot tears.

"Keep searching until sundown. Maybe we can recover his body at sunup," Groman said quietly.

Peregrine nodded and took off into the sky with one flap of her wings. Groman grabbed the tent flap, and after taking a deep breath, he opened the flap and stepped inside.

He saw the rows of wounded Kittrian, Blackmian, Horiton, Amronian, and Flitnao lying in cots and Trodontians hanging in harnesses with healers rushing about tending to them. He looked to his right and noticed a side room that was curtained off. He saw Saralia exit the room, and she noticed him, her eyes widening in horror.

"Please tell me those are not..." she whispered in shock.

"Yes...they are." Groman nodded, setting his jaw in an attempt to keep his tears from falling. "Tell no one about this. Say only to be ready for a gathering of everyone tonight and a meeting with the leaders afterwards, and please find Belinda and Annie and tell them to come here at once."

Saralia's eyes welled up with tears as she rushed out of the tent at a gallop.

Groman took another deep breath and entered Victoria's room. Her armor and weapons had been laid on a table nearby. Victoria herself was standing next to the table, with her back to the door, her long black hair down and looking very disheveled. She was working on taking off the claws on her right arm.

"Are you well?" Groman asked quietly. Victoria didn't turn around.

"I'm fine." Her voice held a cold edge to it as she spoke. "Now, where is my brother, so I can knock some sense into him for sending me away like that?" She turned to face Groman and saw the items he was carrying and the tears flowing down his cheeks. She whipped around quickly and smashed her fists into the table with her weapons and armor.

"He... he can't be..." she whimpered.

"I am so sor—" Groman began, but he was cut off by Victoria spinning around and screaming.

"You took me away from him!"

Groman saw the tips of her claws before he had time to duck; they slashed across his face. Gasping in pain, he stepped back dropping the shirt and bits of metal. Victoria dropped the claws and fell to her knees sobbing. Groman blinked several times and felt his face; he could feel blood running down past his right eye and quickly gathered a bandage from a table and wrapped up the wound.

Just then, Annie burst in, followed by Belinda.

"Where is he?" Belinda asked desperately. She then saw Victoria on the ground in uncontrollable sobs and Groman also fighting back tears as he bandaged his face.

Annie, too, fell to the ground and started crying.

"No...not Stephen..." Belinda whimpered before falling to her knees as well and hugging the two girls.

There, they sat for a few minutes, just crying and holding each other before a sound caught their attention: It was an annoying beeping noise.

"Tori! Your watch!" Annie gasped as she jumped up to retrieve the device.

"Stephen...he's alive!" Victoria grabbed the watch from Annie. Her hands were shaking as she pressed the button. An image of Stephen sitting on a stone wall appeared, and he was looking directly at the group.

"Hello, Tori. If you're seeing this message, that means I had just enough time to have my watch transmit this before I...well, before I died."

"No..." Victoria whimpered again and fell to her knees, while the recording continued.

"After Monaria told us her vision of one of us dying, I had a suspicion it was going to be me, so I wanted to be ready. I wanted to explain some things to you, especially as I probably invoked the 'Excalibur' vow. It's something Groman, and I swore to each other before we left Lulandal the first time. You see, when I watched you get paralyzed from The Shadowed One, the pain I felt for having failed you was just too much to bear, and I know Groman felt something similar with Annie losing her legs. So, we met up after the victory feast and made a vow. Should either one of us be in a position where our life may be ended soon, they need only say 'Excalibur!', and the other is duty bound to get you and Annie out of danger and protected at any cost. I realize now how selfish that may seem, and I can only hope that you haven't been too angry at Groman for what he did. Truth be told, I thought about telling him that he could break the agreement, but I couldn't bring myself to take the chance of you getting hurt again. So here we are. I know this is going to be really hard for you and Belinda, especially after losing Mom and Dad just a month ago, but I know you will be alright eventually. Time helps heal all wounds, as long as they are treated properly. Saralia reminded me of that today. I'm sure you're wondering, 'So now what are we going to do?' Well, do you remember how Monaria repeated herself? I'm positive it means you are going to beat Falron and send him back into whatever dark hole he crawled out of. Just stay together and show him just how strong you really are. I'll be cheering you on with Mom and Dad from up there. I love you, little sis. And yes, I know how much you dislike me saying that, so I'm going to say it again."

The image of Stephen stood up and took a knee in front of Victoria and held out his hand. Victoria quickly put hers to the image.

"Don't ever forget how much I love you, Victoria, and that I'll always have your back. Now, go and live a life just as incredible as the one we've had together. I love you, little sis."

At that, the image froze for a moment before disappearing. Everyone sat in silence for nearly ten minutes, taking in what they had just heard. Then, Victoria's voice broke the silence.

"I won't forget, I...I love you, too, Stephen."

She then stood up and wiped the tears from her face.

"It's time to finish off Falron. Once and for all," she said with pure determination in her voice.

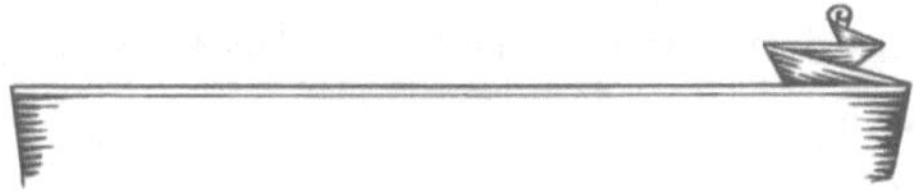

# Chapter 10. Sorrow and Strategy.

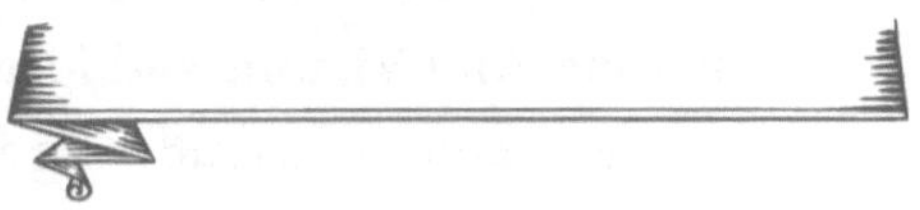

As the last light from the sun disappeared from over the tree tops, the entire camp had been assembled in front of the leader's pavilion, where Groman stood on a large boulder Vesuvian had rolled over.

"People of Lulandal!" he shouted. "It is with a heavy heart that I have summoned you here tonight. We have lost several heroes today. Maku led us to one of the ancient artifacts that may help us win this fight. Droven fought with everything he had and used his training to the fullest; even when faced with innumerable odds, he never stopped fighting until his last breath. And Stephen, the one who has risked his life for our world and peoples time and time again, has fallen."

The people began to murmur and a few even began to cry in despair, but Groman raised his hands for silence.

"But in his dying breath, Stephen did something that will help us end the war! He not only gave us this," Groman held up the other half of the horn of the Horiton, "but in badly wounding Falron and causing him to retreat, he has given us hope! Hope that we can and will defeat this monster and return our world back to the glory it once was! He has paid the price to keep our hopes alive, and we should not take that lightly. In one day's time, we will take the fight to him and end this war once and for all. Are you willing to fight alongside me and take our world back?!"

At this, the people cheered and raised their weapons in the air.

"For Lulandal!" Groman shouted.

"For Lulandal!" The people roared back.

Groman jumped off of the rock and beckoned for the leaders to follow into the pavilion.

"A fine speech, Groman," Elder Gilder said.

"Thank you, Elder," Groman said. "Now, if I can have your attention, please: We need to focus on snuffing out this threat that is Falron the Feared and his army. And Victoria and I have come up with a plan that we hope will bring an end to this suffering and destruction."

"Let us hear it," Chieftain Galent said.

"Firstly, we need to have all the soldiers busying themselves, polishing their armor and weapons. Find every standard and flag you may have, and have the drums of war ready for the coming battle. We want to make this a show of strength in numbers and power. We know that Falron's forces are mostly focused in the south side of Areiop; that area is lower than the rest. We will need to appear on the higher ground to the west at sunrise for maximum effect."

"That sort of thing would be an intimidating force to be sure, but most of Falron's army are shadows. They do not feel fear," Ripper said.

"But the Greatures and Gritters under his command do, and we've seen firsthand how he is unable to control any more people. The more we can thin out of his ranks, the better," Victoria countered.

Ripper nodded his approval, and Groman continued: "When we attack his army, Annie and a small force of Trodontian and Flitnao will charge them from the high ground from the north. There, Annie will use the horn, and regardless of if it works or not, she will double back for her own safety."

"I will carry her into battle myself," a female voice spoke up from behind the group. Everyone turned to see Trinia slowly walking in.

"Are you sure?" Victoria said.

"Quite," Trinia replied firmly.

"Alright. That is settled, then." Groman continued: "The main attack from the west will try to drive a wedge through Falron's forces, straight to Falron himself. Victoria and I will spearhead that assault and deal with him ourselves. From there, it is up to The One Above to decide the outcome."

The leaders whispered among themselves for a few moments and then looked to Groman.

"We will begin preparations right away," Frostous said as he and everyone else left the pavilion, aside from Elder Gilder and Screnlon, who quietly walked over to Victoria and Groman.

"You are worried about this battle, are you not?" Screnlon asked.

"Of course, we are," Victoria replied. "How could we not be?"

Elder Gilder stroked his long white beard and thought for a moment. He then said, "The One Above is in control of this whole war; he will make sure this battle goes the way he wants. Sometimes, it seems we cannot win the war on our own. We need to rely on his strength to carry us through."

"Wise words, to be sure. I hope that winning this war is in The One Above's plan," Groman replied quietly.

"I do not see any reason why he would not want good to prevail over evil," Screnlon said.

Groman and Victoria nodded their agreement, and they left the pavilion.

Victoria caught sight of Trinia standing nearby, facing away from her. Her long tail was low and dragging on the ground, and she could see her shoulders shaking from crying.

"Trinia? Were you waiting for someone?" Victoria asked quietly. Trinia turned to face Victoria with a sorrowful expression.

"Please don't tell me Trakken is..." Victoria began before Trinia cut her off.

"No, he is alive, thanks in no small part to Saralia and Tiny's efforts, but..." she said before breaking down again.

Victoria hurried over to Trinia and hugged her. "It will all be okay no matter what condition he is in," she whispered.

Trinia cried for a few more seconds before she was able to control herself again. "The damage to his hind legs was too severe. Even Tiny in all his Unkarian power cannot cause Trakken's hooves to grow back. He will never be able to use them again," she said weakly.

"I am so sorry," Victoria said quietly. "You know, in my world, I've seen animals that lose their front or back legs receive a wheeled carriage that carries the unusable legs in it, so they can use their good legs to move themselves around. Do you think the blacksmiths can make something like that?"

Trinia managed a weak smile. "They are already beginning to draw up plans to make something for him. I plan to help wherever I can before and after the battle."

"Are you sure you still want to fight?" Victoria asked.

"I am merely taking Annie close to the front lines and then retreating. I may be small, but I should be able to outrun any of his shadows, let alone a Greature or Gritter," Trinia said confidently. "Besides, it is the least I can do after Trakken nearly gave his life for me."

Victoria felt her eyes begin to water again, and this time, it was Trinia who quickly hugged her.

"You have my deepest sympathy for your brother. He was a noble warrior and brave hero. His sacrifice will not be in vain," Trinia said.

"Thank you, Trinia," Victoria whispered.

"Come, allow me to take you to your tent," Trinia said.

"If you insist, though I would prefer to walk," Victoria replied.

"As you wish, my friend," Trinia said with a short laugh as they began walking back to where Victoria was staying.

Later that night, while Victoria was lying in her hammock, she heard a rustle at the tent flap and saw a dark figure enter. She tensed up until she noticed the white fur on the figure's left hand.

"Hannela?" Victoria asked quietly.

"Yes, Victoria, it is I," Hannela replied. "Father wanted to know how you are doing."

"Not good but not terrible, either" Victoria said with a sigh. "I just can't believe I've lost my brother too."

"I wish I could say I understand what you are going through and knew how to help, but I do not," Hannela said as she removed her cloak and weapons before nimbly jumping into her hammock above Victoria.

"That's okay, Hannela," Victoria replied. She then noticed Hannela's black-furred face and yellow eyes peering over the edge of her hammock at her.

"I can at least listen if you want to talk about it."

"I don't know if that will help, either."

"Well, I am not going anywhere until tomorrow morning. If you need someone to talk to, I am here."

"Thank you."

Victoria sighed and pulled the blanket tighter around her, trying to think of something other than the day's events.

"Hey, Hannela?" she asked quietly.

"Yes?" Hannela purred.

"How do you manage to stay calm and collected when you are reacting to an incoming threat?"

"Well, Father always told me to take a breath and analyze the situation, locate the threat, then deal with it accordingly," Hannela replied. "Why do you ask?"

"I think there's something going on with my weapons," Victoria said. "It's hard to describe, but I think I am getting some sort of a boost while wearing them."

Hannela quickly leapt out of her hammock and landed near the table where Victoria had left her weapons. Hannela went to touch the handle but quickly recoiled with a hiss, her ears flat back against her head.

"What was that?!" she asked, surprised.

Victoria got out of her own hammock and picked up one of the claws. Hannela's yellow eyes went wide as she tried to touch the other and again pulled her hand back quickly.

"How..." Hannela began.

"I don't know," Victoria replied quickly. "I really only noticed the effects three days ago."

"This might explain how you were able to move so quickly back in the cave," Hannela mused.

"And why I've been so hesitant to spar with you," Victoria said as she placed the set of claws back on the table. "I was worried I might hurt you."

"Well, I say we find out what they do first thing tomorrow," Hannela said with a yawn. She quickly jumped back into her hammock and looked down at Victoria who was just entering her own.

"Can I ask you a favor?" Victoria asked.

"Of course," Hannela replied.

"Keep this to ourselves. I really don't want any more attention than what I am getting now, especially if I am unable to harness whatever energy is in those blades."

"I will keep that secret with my life," Hannela said. "Now, get some rest. I think we have a lot to do tomorrow."

The next morning, Victoria awoke to a furry hand grasping hers and gently shaking it.

"It is time to get up, Victoria! I have set up a private training ground to find out what your weapons can do!" Hannela purred excitedly.

Victoria groaned, got out of bed, and gathered her claws and gear before following Hannela to a secluded place in the forest. There, she saw over a dozen stalks of what looked like bamboo sticking out of the ground. They were reddish in color, and Victoria could almost swear she could see them visibly growing in front of her. They were over three feet high and still growing.

"Speedwood," Hannela purred happily. "It grows incredibly fast until burned with fire. Kittrian use it for all sorts of buildings and structures. It even comes in different colors. I planted red, so you can see it better against the green foliage."

"So what do you want me to do?" Victoria asked.

"Cut through as many of them as possible in the fastest time," Hannela said. "I will go first to show you." Hannela drew her Katar from their holsters and crouched low. In a flash, she was up and running around, slashing through each stalk with a single, clean, cut. In only a few seconds, she had cut through all of them and was on the other side of the clearing, barely even breathless.

"Seven seconds!" Hannela purred proudly as she made her way back to Victoria. "Not my best time, but I am used to going through less stalks. I wanted to make sure you have plenty to work with."

"You're just showing off," Victoria said as she tightened the straps on her claws.

Hannela smiled and shrugged before gesturing to Victoria to take her turn.

The stalks had nearly grown back to how tall they were before they were cut and made easy targets. Victoria took a breath and lunged forwards, cutting them as fast as she could. By the time she made it through the clearing, she was slightly winded and looked back to see Hannela smiling and holding up two fingers on her right hand and four on her left.

"Twenty-four seconds," Hannela said as Victoria came back to the start. "Not a bad time for a first run. Now, go again, but this time, focus on accuracy. Try to cut them all at the same level."

Victoria tensed her muscles and ran it again, slicing through the stalks with ease.

When she finished and turned around, Hannela called out: "Twenty-three seconds! But your cuts are clean and mostly even, so you are improving!"

"Let me guess, run it again but try for speed?" Victoria asked.

Hannela said nothing but smiled and nodded.

"Okay, then, here I go again," Victoria said as she readied herself for another go. She took a deep breath and focused on the most direct route she was to take. She exhaled and started running; she felt like she wasn't even touching the ground as she slashed through one stalk after another, but right in the middle of her run, she spotted Hannela, weapons drawn, rushing her from her left. Victoria quickly turned and dodged Hannela's attack, giving her a kick in the back as she went by.

Hannela stopped and held up her hands, showing she had placed the Katar back in their holsters. "Good! That was incredibly fast!" she called out. "You nearly outpaced me at my best!"

"Really?" Victoria replied. "You didn't seem to be going that quickly."

"I was sprinting towards you as fast as I could go," Hannela said confused.

"Looked more like a swift jog to me," Victoria retorted.

"Maybe that is what your weapons can do for you, now," Hannela said. "They increase your speed and reaction time."

"Maybe so," Victoria replied. "But we still don't know how or why they have this power."

"Father had a theory he mentioned when he told me about the Broken gauntlets as we used to hide them under the floorboards of our meeting hall back in Felinad: He suspected that certain people who do incredible things may be blessed by The One Above and given abilities that seem supernatural. Or those who are given a seemingly impossible task are granted the power to overcome them in some way, shape, or form," Hannela said.

"That's interesting. We'll have to do some more testing later after we win this fight," Victoria said as she looked down at her claws.

"Agreed, and that being said, I am so excited to see you defeat Falron with those!" Hannela purred happily.

"All I want right now is getting revenge for my brother and this world," Victoria replied coldly.

Hannela's black furred face darkened. "While I can sympathize with you, you must be careful not to be consumed by revenge. We do not want to lose you too," she said softly.

Victoria didn't respond but walked back to camp, where she had breakfast alone before moving on to the healing tent. When she went inside, she saw all of the people lying in beds watching her and murmuring about her and Stephen. A few even tried to sit up and express their condolences, but she quickly told them thanks and that they needed to stay in bed for their own health.

She soon spotted whom she was looking for: Trinia's sleeping form was lying against the heavy curtains of a side room. Victoria quickly got down on the ground next to her and put her hand on Trinia's shoulder.

"Good morning. How is Trakken?" Victoria asked quietly.

Trinia stirred and quickly tried to get to her hooves. "I fell asleep again! I need to check on Trakken!" Trinia said, panicked.

"I am alright, my dear!" Trakken's voice called out from inside the room. "Bring Victoria in with you. I would like to speak to her."

Victoria and Trinia entered the room, and Victoria saw Trakken for the first time since Tiny had carried him away yesterday. From the front, he didn't seem too bad. A few minor burns were healing nicely, but it was his back half that was in rough shape. His hindquarters were hanging by a large harness suspended from the tent roof. He was missing large patches of hair from his hindquarters, his tail was now a mere nub as the hair had burned off, and his legs, which ended just before his hooves, were also badly burned and twisted.

"Hello, Victoria. I apologize for not coming to see you sooner," Trakken said.

"Don't worry about it," Victoria replied. "I can see you're doing better than when we last saw each other."

"Tiny did his best, but not even he can repair all the damage done. Soon, I will have some wheels to help me get around, but my fighting days are over," Trakken said. "But that is not why I wanted you here. Saralia told me about Stephen, and I wanted to give you my deepest sympathy for your loss. He was an incredible warrior and friend, and he will be missed by all."

"Thank you, Trakken," Victoria said quietly, tears welling up in her eyes again. Trinia quickly gripped Victoria and hugged her again.

"We are here for you whenever and however you may need us," Trinia said quietly.

Victoria managed a weak smile before a small figure burst into the room.

"There you are, Victoria! I have been searching the entire camp for you!" Monaria said breathlessly.

"What is it?" Victoria asked.

"He saved them!" Monaria shouted. "He managed to save them!"

"Whom?" Victoria asked.

"The people Falron was controlling! They are returning to the camp unharmed and no longer under Falron's power!"

Trinia and Victoria looked at each other in surprise.

"Groman requests you come at once to the east entrance of the camp!" Monaria said before quickly flying away.

"Follow her!" Trakken said quickly, "Do not worry about me. I will await the story when you return, my dear."

"If you insist," Trinia said before looking to Victoria. "Shall I give you a ride?"

"You're probably faster than me, so let's go!" Victoria said as she hopped onto Trinia's back, and the two took off at a gallop out of the healing tent and towards the east entrance.

They did not have to go far to see the large masses of people from all the tribes and races making their way inside. They looked haggard and weary but joyful to be reunited with family and friends again. Groman was towards the entrance, attempting to direct the crowds to where they needed to go for medical treatment or food.

"The northern healing tent is full! Please make your way to the ones on the south and west sides of the camp! Our food stores are low, but we will make sure all of you are fed and taken care of!" Groman shouted.

The crowds separated as Trinia galloped through them until they reached Groman, who turned to greet them.

"Good morning!" he shouted over the noises of the crowd. "Stephen has given us one more gift! His actions yesterday seem to have broken Falron's hold on the people, and they have all come here seeking refuge."

"How do you know it was Stephen's work?" Victoria asked while still seated on Trinia's back.

"It is only an assumption. When Stephen fought Falron, he was able to not only stab Falron with his dagger, but he also destroyed his left arm with that...whatever that weapon was. Each time he did, some strange purple light burst from the wounds," Groman answered.

Victoria looked over the hundreds of people around them. "Well done, brother," Victoria said under her breath before turning to Groman again. "We should meet up to discuss our battle plans for tomorrow."

"Agreed," Groman responded. "Meet me at my pavilion after the noon meal."

"We will be there," Trinia said before making her way out of the dense crowds. When they had more room to speed up to a trot, Trinia asked, "Where would you like to go, now?"

"Well, I don't want to keep you from Trakken, so why don't we go back there?" Victoria suggested.

"No sooner said than done. Hold on!" Trinia said with a smile as she increased her trot to a gallop.

They were back at the healing tent within minutes. Victoria dismounted from Trinia, and the two walked inside. It was starting to become considerably more crowded than it had been that morning, but all the newcomers seemed so happy to be there among their friends again. Even all the healers seemed to have more energy as they rushed about making sure everyone was taken care of. Trinia and Victoria made their way to where Trakken was to find him waiting with a large wooden box tucked up under his arm.

"I see you have returned, my love," Trakken said with a smile. "By the sounds outside, I assume you have good news?"

"Yes! Stephen's fight yesterday was not in vain! He seems to have freed everyone who was under Falron's control," Victoria said with a smile and a tear in her eye.

"I am glad," Trakken replied. "Falron's power seems to be weakening. I have a feeling that you will defeat him in the field of battle tomorrow."

"Stephen said the same in his last message to me," Victoria said quietly. "I'm still really nervous about it, though."

"And you have every right to be," Trakken said, putting his rough hand on Victoria's shoulder. "You need to rely on The One Above to carry you through this. I have no doubt it is his will for you to succeed tomorrow."

"Thank you, Trakken," Victoria said.

"Now, I have something for you, my dear, that I was saving for our wedding, but you will have better use of it tomorrow," Trakken said, holding out the box to Trinia, who gingerly took it and opened it to reveal a beautiful saber that had been ornately engraved with her name on it. Strangely, it also had some blank spots on the sheath and hilt.

"I left some room for you to add your own touches so that it may indeed be made with both of our love," Trakken said with a grin.

Trinia said nothing but rushed forwards and hugged Trakken as hard as she could.

"Thank you, my dear!" Trinia said with tears in her eyes.

"I know you are not fond of even the thought of fighting, and while I am apprehensive to the thought of you going into battle tomorrow, I know that you will do your best to keep yourself and Annie safe. This blade should help you in that task," Trakken said.

The two lovers stayed in their embrace until the silence was broken by Victoria awkwardly speaking up: "I need to go meet with Groman to discuss the plans for tomorrow in detail. I'll return when we're done to make sure you know what you'll have to do."

"Very well," Trinia replied as she and Trakken separated from their hug. "I will await your return."

Victoria quickly slipped out of the room and out of the healing tent and made her way to the mess hall, where she ate lunch on her own before moving to the pavilion. There, she found Groman, Belinda, Chieftain Galent, Frostous, Vesuvian, Ripper, Screnlon, Vulant, Peregrine, and Elder Gilder looking over a detailed map of Areiop. A dagger had been stuck into the map to signify where Falron's camp was, and some stones had been arranged where the attackers should arrive.

"Are we settled on a battle plan?" Victoria asked as she entered.

"I believe so," Chieftain Galent replied.

"The majority of our army will attack from the west and rush down on Falron's forces. Due his losing most of his possessed army, he will be forced to either rely on the Unkarians, Greatures, and their Gritters to defend him, or he will likely summon as many of his shadow warriors as he can," Groman said.

"He's likely getting desperate by now; he may even use up that ability when he summons them," Belinda added.

"Considering how he loses the power he has stolen from the various artifacts when wounded, he's like a battery that slowly recharges over time. If we push him to his limits, he may burn that ability out," Victoria said.

The leaders looked somewhat confused, but Groman continued: "Then, as the main force charges down the hill, the smaller force of Trodontian and Flitnao warriors will attack from the north, giving Annalio time to blow the Horn of the Horiton. Should it work and summon more warriors to our aid, they will continue their charge into Falron's flank. Annalio and Trinia will have retreated to the top of the ridge by this time to keep the two of them safe." Groman looked at Victoria before continuing. "You and I will stay on the front lines as much as possible until we see an opportunity to strike at Falron, in which case we are to throw everything at him we can. If that does not happen, and he prefers to stay out of the battle, Belinda will try to draw him out with her armor."

"I just hope the firebreak armor can still take the heat," Belinda commented.

"Should we be able to confront Falron, we are to use every ability we have to defeat him and secure the victory," Groman finished.

The leaders nodded their agreement and looked to Groman, who dismissed them with a wave of his hand.

As they filed out, Groman looked at the map and sighed. "This is it, is it not? Our final battle against this evil?"

"Let's hope that when Falron is defeated, this world will receive its much-needed peace and prosperity," Belinda commented as she left the pavilion.

Victoria walked over to Groman and stood next to him. "Groman, may I ask you a question?" she asked quietly.

"Of course," Groman said without looking up from the map.

"What are you going to do after you win this war?"

Groman straightened up and looked at Victoria with slight confusion.

"I...do not know," he answered hesitantly, "I wish I could stop being the chosen one and become a master healer and spend my life helping people."

"That's all?" Victoria asked.

"Well...should I find the right woman, I would like to start a family someday, but I do not know who would be willing to take in someone such as myself," Groman answered.

"Have you ever met someone like that?"

"I once thought I did. She was a wonderful woman; beautiful, intelligent, kind, gentle, but also brave and courageous."

"Have you tried to talk to her?"

Groman sighed and looked at the map again. "I have come to the realization that while I may think we are meant for each other, we are...worlds apart, and our bond is not meant to be."

Victoria looked towards the tent flap and was about to leave when Groman spoke behind her.

"What about you? What do you think you will do when this is over?"

Victoria thought for a moment and looked at the ground. "I'm not sure anymore. With Mom, Dad, and Stephen gone, I'm not sure what I will do. Maybe I'll try to start a business or find a man to marry and settle down with to start a family. I'm not sure, really."

"Both sound like good options."

"Yeah...honestly, the first one is more likely."

"You do not think you will meet someone to marry?"

"I thought I did...once, but it was like you said, I realized we were worlds apart, and it would never work out between us."

"I am sorry to hear that."

Victoria sighed and looked back at Groman. She saw again the bandage over his eye and felt her face turn red with shame.

"Groman, I just wanted to say I'm sorry for what..." she began.

But Groman cut her off: "No apologies are necessary, my friend. You were in emotional pain and were not in full control of your actions. Nobody blames you for what happens, myself included."

"But there's one more thing."

"Oh?"

"I...I think my claws have become like the ancient artifacts."

"How do you mean?"

"When I wear them, I feel like time is slowing down, and I am able to move faster than I have thought possible. I've been struggling to control myself ever since; when you told me the news, I still had one claw on, and the emotions made me lose control, and...."

"I see. I knew you did not do it on purpose."

"I admit in the moment I was going to slap you. I just forgot I was still armed."

"What has passed has passed. And much as I would like to discuss this further, we do have a battle to prepare for."

"Of course," Victoria replied. "I'm going to go make sure my gear is ready."

The rest of the afternoon and into the evening was spent sharpening blades, cleaning weapons and armor, and making any adjustments needed for the next morning. Victoria kept herself busy making sure she had everything she needed for the battle ahead.

That evening, she was lying in her hammock and trying to get some sleep when she rolled over and felt something in her pocket. She reached inside and pulled out the picture of her and her family at the state park. She thought back to that day: They had arrived in the morning to rain, which soon let up, only to be replaced by swarms of mosquitoes all afternoon. Yet that wasn't the part she remembered from that trip; it was when that picture had been taken. They had arrived back at their car in the parking lot when her mom pointed out the breathtaking sunset, and they had all posed for the picture. Nobody complained about the rain or the bugs; they were just all happy to be there together.

"Now, there's only one of us left," Victoria said softly to herself.

Just then, she spotted a rustling at the tent flap, and Hannela entered. She walked over to the table and removed her armor and weapons before turning back to Victoria.

"Is that a portrait of your family?" she asked quietly.

"Yeah. It's a picture we took while on a trip a few years ago," Victoria replied as she held it out for Hannela to look at.

Hannela gingerly took it and examined it. "It looks so lifelike; it is as if I am looking at that exact moment!" Hannela said in shock.

"In my world, we have things like my watch that can take a picture of anything we want, so we can remember the moment."

"That is truly incredible!" Hannela said as she handed the picture back to Victoria. She then leapt up to her hammock and was soon asleep.

Victoria soon followed her to slumber, knowing that the battle would soon come.

# Chapter 11. Going all in.

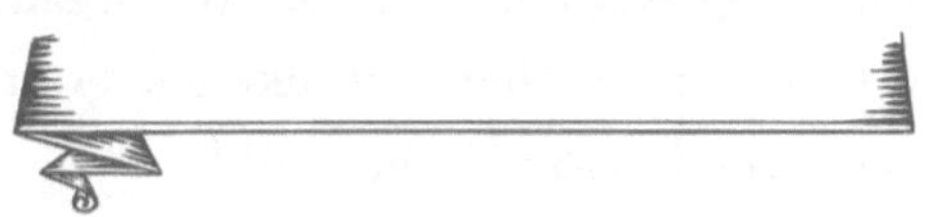

The morning sun broke through the burned trees as a Greature sprinted through Falron's camp, screaming: "To arms! To arms! The enemy is coming!"

He soon reached the empty shell that had once been the great hall and began pounding on the door will all his strength, only to have the doors break free from their hinges and fall to the ground inside, revealing Falron lying on the bed, being attended to by several Greature healers. He looked at the Greature who had just burst in with an angry stare.

"Pardon the intrusion, sire, but the army of Lulandal are here! They are going to attack!" the Greature panted.

"What?" Falron said as he got up from his bed and made his way outside. He blinked from the bright sunlight and saw it all: the Unkarian and Greature armies scrambling to gather their weapons, while warning horns sounded. Gritters darted everywhere until they came under the control of a Greature, then they quickly sprinted to their side.

But it was what he saw on the ridge that caught Falron's attention: It was a massive army of Kittrian, Trodontian, Ice Dwarf, Fire Giant, and Amronian troops numbering in the thousands, their armor and weapons gleaming in the morning sun, standards and battle flags held high, and war drums causing the very air to shake to their rhythm.

Up on the ridgeline, Groman was riding on Chieftain Galent's back as the two were running along the line of soldiers, and Groman was shouting to the assembled armies.

"People of Lulandal! I call on you now! Whether you be Kittrian, Trodontian, Horiton, Unkarian, Flitnao, Amronian, Blackmian, or Human, we need to stand together and take back our home! Are you with me?!" Groman yelled as loud as he could.

"We are with you!" came the deafening reply.

Falron looked at the Greature, who was shaking in fear.

"What are we to do, sire?! We are outnumbered!" the Greature said in a panic.

"Not for long," Falron said as he raised his right arm and his left stump, his eyes turned violet, and a dark energy surged from him.

On the ridgeline, the army of Lulandal watched as legions of shadow warriors of all shapes and sizes appeared in full battle array.

Back at the camp, Falron fell to his knees and gasped in pain.

"My lord! What are your orders?" the Greature asked.

"Protect me and this building at all costs. Now, your numbers far surpass theirs. I have no interest in prisoners, now. Kill them all for all I care," Falron said as he went back inside the ruined great hall.

The Greature let loose a roar that was soon echoed by all the other living troops, and the shadows shrieked in reply as they surged towards the army.

"Here they come," Victoria said as she sat atop Saralia. She looked over in the distance and could see Annie, Trinia, and their small group assembling on the north ridge.

Groman atop of Galent turned to face the oncoming horde, their swords raised. "Now is the time to fight!" Groman shouted. "For The One Above!"

"For The One Above!" the army shouted in reply.

"For Lulandal!" Groman shouted.

"For Lulandal!" the echo came all throughout the army.

"And for Stephen!" Victoria shouted.

"For Stephen!" the reply rang out in Victoria's ears as the army surged forwards as one like a wave racing towards a beach.

The sky over them was darkened as hundreds of Blackmian and Horiton warriors soared overhead towards the enemy, and hundreds of their shadow doppelgangers took to the skies from the enemy camp as well. The airborne warriors started to fire arrows into the opposing sides, with each putting up shields to try and block the attack.

Victoria closed the visor on her helmet and gripped Saralia's flanks with her knees as tightly as she could, as the wave of enemies came closer and closer. *Watch my back, Stephen*, she thought as they galloped ahead.

Meanwhile, on the north ridge, Annie and her group were standing by, watching the initial charge.

"It's now or never, everyone!" Annie shouted as loud as she could.

"For The One Above!" Windmere's loud voice boomed as she reared up on her hind legs.

"For Lulandal!" Urano shouted as he lowered his sword and flew forwards towards the enemy with the two dozen Flitnao following him.

"For Stephen!" Annie and Trinia shouted in unison as they and the five other Trodontian warriors galloped ahead.

When they had gotten halfway towards the enemy lines, Windmere looked back at Annie and shouted, "Blow the horn!"

Annie put the horn to her lips and blew as hard as she could. A sweet but piercing sound echoed around the valley.

*"Who do you call?"* a voice quietly asked in Annie's head.

*I call all allies of Lulandal to come and fight for our future and our home!* Annie thought.

*"Very well,"* the voice replied from within.

Annie looked around her at the Trodontians surrounding her and the Flitnao overhead.

"Did anything happen?" she asked.

It looked like Windmere was about to reply when the sky began to darken over them. Annie quickly looked up and saw thousands of Flitnao warriors above and around them, weapons ready and eyes set on the enemy.

"All of my people are here!" Monaria called out as she flew alongside Annie and Trinia.

Suddenly, loud screams echoed around them, and Annie spotted hundreds of white furred figures with black horns carrying spears and pikes sprinting behind them.

"The Ibexian army is here too!" Annie called out.

"Annie! It is time for you to turn back!" Windmere shouted back.

Trinia nodded, swiftly turned around, and galloped back to the top of the ridge, dodging their newly arrived allies as they went. When they reached the top of the ridge, they continued towards where the other army had started their own charge.

Meanwhile, the other army was nearly at the enemy, spears and pikes lowered and swords, war hammers, and axes raised as the two came closer. Saralia drew her bow and began loosing arrows into the horde of shadows as they overtook the Greatures and Gritters, as many other archers did the same.

The two armies closed, two hundred yards, then one hundred; now, only fifty yards. Victoria braced herself for impact.

The two armies hit each other like freight trains in a head-on collision, but the grand army of Lulandal pushed through and began fighting the shadows on all sides. It was pure chaos. Victoria swiped at a Greature who had gotten too close with a lance, only to be knocked off Saralia's back by a different Greature with a club.

"Tori!" Saralia shouted as she slashed through the Greature with her scimitars.

"I'm fine!" Victoria shouted back as she got to her feet and sprinted towards the enemy. "Just remember the goal! Keep pressing on to where Falron is!"

Victoria heard a chorus of shrieks and growls as nearly two dozen gritters raced towards her. She held her claws out and rushed towards them shrieking a battle cry.

"For my brother!" she screamed as she quickly took them all out, cutting them to ribbons.

Suddenly, a torrent of flame came from above them and torched some of their airborne allies.

"That was no fire giant!" Groman shouted, pointing his sword at the ruined great hall.

"Leave him to me!" Belinda said as she ran towards the flames waving her black sword and large shield. "Over here, you stupid wizard wannabe! You want a target?! I'm right here!"

Victoria watched her aunt fully clad in black and red plate armor with a flowing reddish-black cape stopped nearly two hundred feet from the great hall. Falron was on top of the roof looking at her. He seemed to ignore her until nearly a dozen other soldiers surrounded her and also started taunting him.

"Go away!" Belinda shouted at them. "If he torches me, you'll all be dead!"

But it was too late. A wave of fire blasted the area where she stood. Belinda closed the slits in her visor and held her shield in front of her as she heard the screams from the other soldiers around her. The air grew hotter and hotter before letting up.

Victoria saw it all: The soldiers were there one moment; then just piles of molten metal and ash the next. She saw Belinda on a knee with her shield in front of her, both her armor and shield were red hot, but, to Victoria's shock, Belinda stood up and held her sword out in front of her.

"You call that hot?!" Belinda bellowed from inside her helmet. "I've endured fire giant farts worse than that!"

Falron seemed to get visibly angry, and this time, he let loose a torrent of blue fire at Belinda who again placed her shield in front of her and seemed to disappear within the flames.

On the north flank, Windmere led the enlarged army through the city ruins and towards the enemy's right flank. She saw that they had somehow not noticed them yet and quickened her pace. "Brace yourselves!" she shouted as she raised her two great swords and then smashed into the column of shadows who had just now saw them and were turning to meet them.

The Trodontians acted like a wedge and smashed their way through the enemy lines as the Flitnao zipped around, slashing anyone within reach and staying away from enemy blades. The Ibexians came right on the heels of the Trodontian advance and literally butted their way in, using their long horns to skewer any enemy in their way before swinging their spears and pikes to clear a path through.

Belinda began to feel the air lessen as the fire burned around her but she held firm. After nearly two minutes of flame, the heat let up, and Belinda released her grip on the visor letting the slits open again and precious air in. She looked up to see Falron had fallen to his knees on the rooftop. "You're just not hot enough to fry Belinda the Brave!"

she taunted again, banging her sword against her shield, the red hot metal causing sparks to fly with each impact. She squinted at Falron who was back on his feet and putting his right hand against the stump of his left arm and seemed to be screaming something as his eyes visibly glowed red.

Another torrent of fire came at her, and again, she took a knee and held her shield in front of her, but this time, the flames seemed different.

Victoria slashed her way through some Greatures as she felt the air around her get hot. She looked back at where Belinda was and to her horror watched as the flames seemed to tighten around themselves and shrink into a white-hot beam that hit Belinda's shield and began to push her back through the dirt.

Belinda could feel the intense heat begin to melt through her shield as she was sliding backwards. She put her right arm in front of her face just as the shield gave out and broke into two pieces. She quickly moved her left arm in front of her face as well. The heat was literally taking her breath away as she screamed in pain.

"Aunt Belinda, no!" Victoria screamed as she watched her aunt lose her footing and tumble backwards into a ruined house. Then, the beam stopped, and Victoria saw that Falron had nearly fallen off the roof, only to be caught by a Greature and taken back inside the hall.

"A little help?!" Belinda's voice rang out from inside her helmet.

Victoria ran towards her but saw Vesuvian get there first as he knocked the rubble away and picked up Belinda in his huge hand before setting her back on the ground. Her armor was glowing red and visibly steaming, plus her arm guards were slightly melted, but she was alright. She drew her sword again and looked at where Falron had been.

"I think you really took it out of him!" Victoria called out.

"You did well," Vesuvian said as he turned towards the horde of enemies rapidly approaching them.

"Don't congratulate me yet!" Belinda said as she slowly marched forwards towards a Greature who swung his club at her. She dodged it and dropped her sword, only to bear hug the Greature with her red-hot armor. The Greature screamed in pain before she let it go, picked up her sword, and swiftly ended it. "Keep pushing on!" she yelled to Victoria. "Don't wait for us! Go get that man and show him what happens when he messes with our family!"

Victoria nodded and looked at some shadow archers who were aiming at her. "Not this time, you won't!" she called out before taking a deep breath and watching as the arrows moved towards her in slow motion. She easily dodged each one and descended on the archers with a fury few can know and survive.

After dispatching them, Victoria surveyed the battlefield around her. Her allies were desperately fighting the hordes of shadows, while Greatures and Gritters were scattered everywhere, many of whom lay dead or dying on the ground. Groman had gotten knocked off Chieftain Galent and was busy cleaving an evil Unkarian in half with one swing of the massive Empty Sword. Saralia had more than a few scratches on her flanks but was busy cutting her way through the enemies with her scimitars.

Victoria heard screaming coming from her left and spotted Greatures and Gritters running for their lives as thousands of Flitnao descended on them, followed by Windmere and hundreds of Ibexians.

"The horn worked!" Victoria shouted in jubilation.

"Time for you to face Falron at the great hall!" Windmere said as she knocked aside a fleeing greature.

"I'd love to, but we still have a lot of enemies to get through!" Victoria said as she quickly slashed through another group of gritters.

"Tiny clear path!" Tiny roared as he rushed into the fray, holding what looked like a large table like a snowplow and smashing his way through the shadows.

"Keep the enemies from closing in on him!" Groman shouted as he followed behind Tiny.

Victoria picked up her pace and rushed in behind Groman and Tiny. "I've got your backs!" she shouted as she slashed away at a shadow Trodontian who was rushing in.

Soon, they came to the ruins of the great hall, and Tiny picked up the table and threw it at the Greatures in front of the door, causing them to scatter in fear. The table smashed through the doors, leaving an opening for Groman and Victoria to enter. "Little heroes go inside. Deal with bad man. Tiny stay outside and keep pests busy," Tiny ordered. Groman and Victoria looked at each other and, with grim determination, stepped inside the hall.

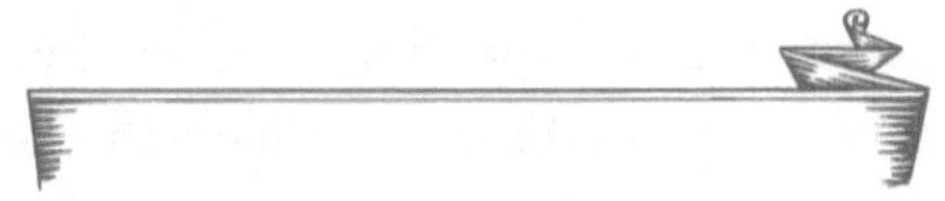

# Chapter 12. Confrontation.

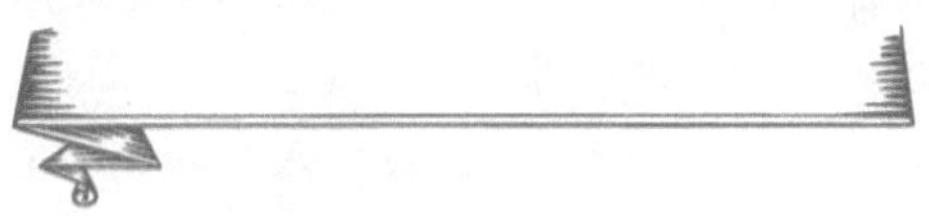

Victoria slowly stepped inside what was left of the great hall. She had never been inside it before, and she could tell it used to be a massive building. The wood beams that held up the ceiling were easily three feet in diameter, and all the wood was ornately carved with the symbols of the different tribes to show their unity in defeating The Shadowed One.

The two warriors scanned the dim light, trying to find where Falron was, when they heard a voice coming from the darkness.

"So you've finally come to kill me. Is that it?" Falron asked. His voice seemed to come from everywhere and echoed around the massive room.

"Yes," Victoria said coldly.

Falron laughed. "So no mercy, eh? That's a surprise coming from the 'good guys.' What if I surrendered and told my army to stand down? What would you do, then?"

"If...if you surrender, you will be given a fair trial, and justice for your crimes will be done," Groman replied hesitantly.

"Ah, but that's not what either of you want, is it? Especially after I killed your friends and family," Falron laughed again. "The mere fact that you are here after so much has happened to you and your friends means you won't give up easily. Which is good; I and my friends here will have a glorious fight!"

A spurt of flame went out from one of the ceiling beams and into a trough of oil that went around the entire hall. The oil quickly ignited and revealed over a hundred Greatures clad in heavy plate armor and wielding massive pikes, spears, war hammers, and maces. The Greatures all started roaring and preparing to fight, as Groman and Victoria looked on in fear.

"You see, I've kept the best for last! A full unit of Greature elites ready to counterattack your weakening army, who are still trying to deal with all the shadow warriors I've summoned!" Falron laughed as he appeared from behind a roof truss. He then looked down at the awaiting soldiers. "Go! Smash what is left of their army, take no prisoners, and keep all the loot for yourselves! Just leave those two to me."

The Greature elites charged towards a wall and quickly smashed through it and out into the battlefield.

Outside, Tiny had just stomped some gritters into the ground when he heard the roars coming from inside. He turned just in time to see the wave of elites crash through the wall and rush towards the allied army. Tiny let out his own roar as he rushed towards the elites; two of whom turned to face him and charged. Tiny didn't even slow down as he hit them with a powerful backhand, knocking them into the wall, and before they could get up, Tiny squished their helmets like one would crush a soda can with his massive fists.

Belinda had just stopped to catch her breath when something hard hit the side of her helmet and knocked her to the ground. Dazed, she looked up to see one of the elites standing over her with his war hammer, ready to swing again, when a deafening boom was heard. The elite swayed a bit on his feet and then fell backwards, a new hole having appeared on his helmet.

Several more booms were heard, and Belinda realized what they were.

*Gunshots?* she wondered as a shadow fell over her.

"Take my hand!" a masculine voice shouted over more gunshots.

"We've got more hostiles coming from the right flank!" the voice of a young woman echoed in Belinda's helmet. She felt a strong arm pull her to her feet, and she lifted the visor to see two people who were very out of place on this battlefield.

A young man and woman dressed like anyone else from Earth but also wearing full tactical gear and wielding firearms were busy driving off the elites from their immediate area. The young man was using a large lever action rifle to punch holes in the elite's armor, while another more modern rifle was on his back, and a large handgun sat in a holster on his belt. He had dark brown hair that was barely visible under a baseball cap and was just over six feet tall. The young woman was using a more compact rifle and also had two pistols in holsters on her belt, one on each side. She had long blond hair in a ponytail sticking out under her own baseball cap and was much shorter than the man at just over five feet tall.

"Miss Belinda, are you alright?" the young woman asked.

"I've felt worse. Is that you, Dani?" Belinda asked.

The young woman smiled. "Yup! You wouldn't believe how we got here, either!" Dani said as she reloaded her rifle.

"It was the strangest thing!" the man Belinda now knew was Jack Briggs said as he switched to his modern rifle and continued firing on the elites. "We were just getting set up for a morning of target practice, and we both heard Annie's voice saying to prepare to fight for our friends in Lulandal."

"You're forgetting the part where you were about to propose to me before we heard the voice," Dani said with a giggle.

Jack's face turned red as he quickly raised his rifle and dropped another elite who was sneaking up behind Belinda with several well-aimed shots.

"Anyway, after we heard Annie's voice, this golden portal opened up, and we could see your army charging into battle, so we gathered up what we had and ran in to help you!" Dani said as she reloaded her rifle again.

"You never gave me your answer though, dear," Jack said as he dropped his rifle and drew his pistol to deal with some Gritters who were swarming them. After emptying his magazine, Jack took a few steps back to reload, and Belinda rushed in with her sword, quickly cutting up the remaining enemies.

"You really want me to answer that now?!" Dani shouted. Just then, her rifle jammed, and she struggled to clear it. Suddenly, four more elites charged in, roaring like a freight train at high speed. "Cover me, Jack!"

"Copy that!" Jack replied as he quickly drew his lever action rifle again and started blasting away, quickly dropping the four attackers. He looked at Belinda and patted the rifle stock. "Old western buffalo gun; forty-five-ninety caliber. There's little armor that can stand up to this old gem."

"Yes!" Dani said as she cleared the jam and turned to face Jack.

"What?" Jack asked.

"Yes, I'll marry you, Jack Briggs!" Dani replied with a grin as she quickly turned to shoot at some shadow Blackmians who were swooping low to attack.

"Danielle Wyng, you've made me a very happy man!" Jack said with a shout.

Belinda stared at the two young people, rolled her eyes, lowered her visor and quickly got to work slashing away at some more Gritters.

"Belinda, where's Stephen and Victoria?" Dani shouted over the gunfire.

Belinda froze before responding: "Victoria and Groman are facing down Falron as we speak."

"And Stephen?" Jack asked.

Belinda said nothing but kept fighting.

A look of understanding and sorrow came over Jack's face as he kept shooting at the enemy. "I have no doubt he died a hero so that you all could fight another day," he said.

"That he did," Belinda said grimly. "Now, we need to keep fighting so that Groman and Victoria can deal with that scoundrel inside the great hall!"

As the chaos continued outside the hall, inside, it was strangely quiet as Falron's voice continued to echo around Groman and Victoria: "I think I am really going to enjoy ruling this world. I've spent enough time here to appreciate what it has to offer."

"How long have you been here?" Victoria asked. She was trying to figure out where Falron was by tracking his voice, and she knew she needed to keep him talking.

"What year is it on Earth?" Falron asked. "I assume it's not nineteen fifty-six anymore?"

"No, we're in the twenty-first century, now," Victoria responded. "How have you managed to stay alive so long?"

"I don't know," Falron said with a laugh. "Maybe all this power is keeping me alive. It gives me all the more reason to take it."

"Why do you think you need to rule my world?" Groman asked.

"Why, it is my destiny!" Falron replied. "Both of my parents told me that I was a part of the master race and that it is my destiny to rule others."

"Oh, terrific, he's a neo-Nazi," Victoria groaned.

"No comments from the peanut gallery!" Falron screamed from the shadows above them. "You wanted to know why I am destined to rule? Then, let me tell you! When I was younger, I even tried to lead my hometown to prosperity. Well, the man who called himself the mayor didn't like that and had me thrown in prison because he was scared of my superiority. I escaped and ran into the woods to make a new plan."

"That's when I found myself here. I decided to learn from my past experiences and observed the tribes here to better find a way to control them when I was taken captive by some monsters from over the sea. After slaving away for a few years and planning a way to rule, I finally escaped with the help of a loyal follower and then made my way back here and began to enact my plan to take over this world. Sure, I had some setbacks; that stupid Unkarian calling himself 'The Shadowed One' didn't help me any, but I learned that I needed to make sure my followers were totally under my control before sending them after artifacts. And now...." Falron jumped down to face the two heroes, his lean body illuminated by the fires above them. He was wearing no armor, not even a shirt; just his ragged black-and-white-striped pants, and he had a simple one-handed sword in his right hand. "...We're here. Alright then, who wants to strike the first blow?" he asked as he slowly walked around Groman and Victoria who held their position but kept turning so they always faced him.

Suddenly, Falron's black eyes turned green, and he vanished from view.

"Where did he go?!" Groman shouted as he frantically looked around.

"Ready or not! Here I come!" Falron's voice echoed from all around the two fighters.

Suddenly, they heard Falron's nearly manic scream as he lunged at them from the shadows. Groman deftly blocked the attack with his blade, and before Victoria could get in a counterattack, Falron had vanished again.

"Oh! Looks like you were ready! Maybe I shouldn't be so noisy this time," Falron's voice seemed to come from everywhere.

"Back-to-back!" Victoria quickly said to Groman.

Just as they were getting into position, Falron lunged at Victoria. He swung his sword low, and Victoria quickly leapt out of the way, but the blade scratched Groman's legs, causing him to grunt in pain.

"I got first blood!" Falron laughed before vanishing again.

"We have to figure out where he will show up next!" Groman shouted as he quickly scanned the room.

Hannela's voice suddenly echoed through Victoria's mind: *Father always told me to take a breath and analyze the situation. Locate the threat and then deal with it accordingly.*

She took a deep breath, then looked around. She didn't see anything at first but then noticed a green blur moving towards them. It was Falron running at a pace she had never seen before. She quickly charged at him with a shriek and was surprised to see the utter shock on his face.

"How...are...you...?" Falron's voice asked in slow motion as she kicked him in the gut, sending him sprawling to the ground.

"I've gotten better since the last time we fought," Victoria said coldly. She rushed at him again, this time with her claws in position to skewer him, but he vanished again.

"How did you get over there?!" Groman shouted.

Victoria looked, and, to her amazement, she was on the other side of the hall.

Just then, Falron appeared behind Groman, and, to her horror, he had appeared with his blade sticking through Groman's chest. Groman's eyes went wide as Falron laughed and disappeared again.

"No!" Victoria screamed as she sprinted towards Groman.

"Stop, Victoria!" Groman called back. "He missed my body but only just. Focus on finding him again!"

Victoria stopped running and inhaled again and looked around. This time, she spotted Falron sprinting towards her, and she quickly braced herself for the attack. His sword came down and clashed with her claws, and the two were face to face.

"I see you've gotten an upgrade! I'll have to try that power for myself!" Falron said as he tried to touch the blades with the stump of his left arm. Victoria quickly pulled the claws back, cutting the stump, and Falron shrieked in pain. A violet light glowed from the wound and suddenly burst out like a small explosion.

"No! Not again!" Falron screamed. He looked at Victoria and Groman, and a crazed-yet-cruel expression came over his face. "That's it. No more easy mode. That sword and its power will be mine!" Then, he vanished yet again.

Victoria took a breath and looked around, and she saw a green blur two inches from her face. Falron's sucker punch sent her spinning to the ground in a daze. She tried to get up, but he appeared in front of her and kicked her hard in the chest: once, twice; three times. She gasped for air, blood dripping from her mouth.

Groman rushed in, screaming: "Leave her alone!" He lowered the Empty Sword and tried to run Falron through, but, at the last second, Falron turned his body sideways and caught the blade between his right arm and his side.

"No..." Victoria weakly gasped as she and Groman both saw the sheen of the Empty Sword begin to dim, and Groman struggled to pull it away.

"Learned that trick from your brother," Falron said with a cruel smile. "Now, all this power will be mine!"

Groman gave his sword one last tug, and he managed to pull it away from Falron. But it seemed to be too late. The sword was now dull and grey, and Falron's eyes began to glow with a golden light. To Victoria's horror, he began to float off the ground.

"Ah, yes! I can feel it!" Falron shouted. "After all I've been through! The imprisonment here and Earth, the slavery, and toil; the backstabbing! I finally have all the power I need to rule this world and Earth! It's all at my fingertips!"

Victoria staggered to her feet and looked at Falron with defiance in her eyes. "My weapons have power too! Don't you want to come get them?!" she shouted.

"Hmm, let me think about it," Falron said, rubbing his chin. "Nah."

All at once, Falron swooped down and punched Groman in the face, the impact sending him flying across the room and into the wall.

"Groman!" Victoria shouted.

"Your turn!" Falron replied with a laugh as he spun around and backhanded her into a table. Victoria tried to get to her feet but fell on her hands and knees, coughing up more blood. "Hah! This is too fun!" Falron said. "Perhaps I should let some of your friends in here, so I can get some entertainment from them too...."

Groman got to his feet and sprinted towards Falron again, holding the Empty Sword low until he was close enough to swing for Falron's head. Falron merely caught the blade with his bare hand.

"Foolish boy. I have the same power as this sword once did. I can do anything it could," Falron said before launching into a series of punches into Groman's chest plate, causing a serious dent to form. Groman grunted in pain and tried to smash Falron's head with both fists locked together. Falron caught the blow with his hand and Groman looked in horror as the Broken Gauntlets were drained of their power and turned to dust. Falron quickly punched Groman in the stomach again, causing him to fall backwards to the ground.

"Thanks for the boost. Now, go back to your corner," Falron said as he swiftly kicked Groman in the gut, sending him back into the same wall where he was to begin with. "Now, my little lady friend, let's see about those claws." He slowly walked over to where Victoria was still struggling to get to her feet, blood dripping from her mouth.

Groman closed his eyes and winced in pain. *Oh, One Above, I cannot do this. I cannot win this fight. Even if it may cost my life, please let me save my sister and my friends*, he prayed.

Suddenly, the sound of a metal object hitting the wood floor was heard. Falron was about to grasp Victoria's claws when he heard the noise and turned to see what had caused it.

Groman gasped as he saw what it was: The Servant's Sword had separated from The Empty Sword and clattered to the ground.

"Hmm. It looks like even your god abandoned you," Falron said as he turned back to Victoria.

Groman shut his eyes in pain again and prayed: *One Above, please do not leave me! Please lend me your power to save the one I love!*

*You already have the power you need,* a still small voice replied in his mind. *You need only reach out and accept it.*

Groman felt a familiar sensation near him. He reached out his right hand, and Falron froze, his hand inches from Victoria's weapons, his eyes wide in shock.

Victoria watched as Falron began to slowly slide backwards towards Groman's outstretched hand.

"What?!" Falron asked in surprise. "How?!"

"You took my sword and its power," Groman said as he grasped the Servant's Sword in his left hand and continued to hold out his right. "That means I can summon you like I could summon my sword!"

"No! No! No!" Falron shrieked. "I won't go out like this!" He grasped a wooden support post and held on tightly with his one good arm. "I refuse to be summoned to your hand like some magic trinket!" Suddenly, the sound of metal cutting through flesh was heard, and Falron saw his one remaining hand fall to the ground. He looked up to see Victoria, her claws lowered, swinging for his chest, but before her blades connected, he felt himself flying through the air and towards Groman's right hand. "This cannot be possible!" Falron screamed as he neared Groman.

Then, it happened: Groman caught Falron by the throat with his right hand, while his left drove the Servant's sword through Falron's heart. A second later, Groman released his grip on Falron and pulled the sword from his chest. Falron staggered backwards as red, gold, and green light began to expand from the wounds in his chest and arms like an egg slowly cracking.

"You fools!" Falron shrieked in fear. "Do you know what you've done?!"

Suddenly, Falron screamed as the light quickly overcame him and burst out in every direction, tearing through the wooden beams like paper.

Outside, the allied army had finished off the last Greature elite and were now looking around for any more threats when Windmere's voice was heard shouting.

"Fall back! Fall back! The great hall is collapsing!" she screamed as she quickly galloped away.

The other soldiers looked and saw a bright burst of multicolored light explode from the great hall and rapidly expand outwards in all directions. Everyone didn't hesitate but ran as fast as they could to get away from the explosion. They quickly neared the outskirts of the battlefield and turned back. The energy explosion had dissipated, and they could clearly see the remains of what was once the great hall. It had collapsed on itself as if someone had knocked its walls in and the roof simply fell on top. A quiet but horrifying revelation came over everyone.

"Groman..." Windmere said in shock.

"Victoria..." Belinda's voice shook in fear.

"Do you think they're...?" Jack asked quietly.

"I... I do not know," Monaria replied.

Suddenly, a beam of golden light burst through the roof and towards the sky for a few seconds before flickering and going out.

"That's them!" Annie shouted as she and Trinia galloped over.

"You heard her!" Chieftain Galent's voice boomed. "Let us go and rescue our heroes!"

The army quickly rushed towards the rubble and started digging through the piles of splintered wood. They found Groman first; he was badly bruised but still breathing, and underneath him was Victoria, unconscious and injured but still alive.

As their rescuers pulled them out, Groman broke free from their grip and started digging through the rubble.

"Wait! We cannot leave them buried," he said. Soon, he found what he was looking for: two pieces of shiny metal, the Servant's Sword and The Empty Sword.

# Chapter 13. Farewell.

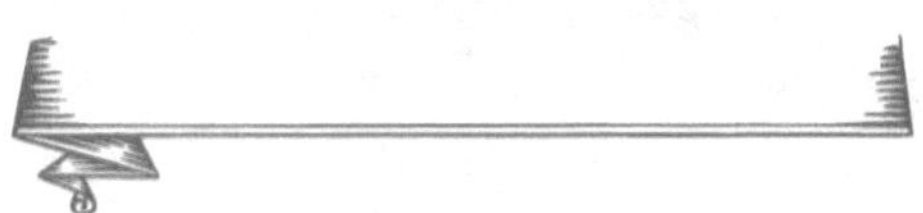

Victoria awoke in a bed in the healing tent to Tiny standing over her. He swayed on his feet a little before giving her a big smile and passing out onto the ground with a tremendous *thud* that shook not only her bed but all the others as well.

"Thank you again, Tiny," Victoria said softly as she looked over the now-sleeping giant. She slowly got out of bed and out of her room into the main tent and then outside into the early evening air. As soon as she was outside, she was engulfed in a hug from several familiar people.

"You did it, Tori!" Annie said excitedly.

"I knew you would win," Belinda added.

"Well done, soldier," Jack said.

"Stephen would be proud," Dani chimed in.

Victoria felt her eyes begin to water again as even more people joined in the group hug.

"You did it, my friend!" Saralia said.

"You are truly incredible!" Trinia said.

"I am glad to see your training paid off," Hannela purred.

"You saved the world once again," Windmere added.

"You and your brother are both heroes," Monaria whispered in Victoria's ear.

"Um...can I just get some air?" Victoria said quietly.

Everyone let her go and stepped back to give her some space. Victoria looked around at all her friends.

"Jack Briggs? Dani Wyng?" Victoria asked in surprise.

"That's soon to be Mrs. Briggs," Dani replied with a giggle.

"How did you get here?" Victoria asked.

"The Horn of the Horiton," Jack answered.

Victoria thought about it for a moment before her eyes went wide. "Wait!" she said. "You're getting married?"

"Yup!" Dani giggled.

"Where's the ring?" Victoria asked.

Jack sheepishly pulled out a smashed jewelry box from his pocket. "I got hit by a really big club during the battle. My body armor took most of the hit, but sadly, the ring was broken too."

"You need a ring?" Trinia quickly interjected. "I can try to fix yours or make you a new one tonight."

"That would be great! Thanks!" Jack said.

"Just come with me to my tent, and I will get started right away!" Trinia said as the three of them walked away.

"I'm glad that worked out," Belinda said. "You should have heard him when he realized what had happened. I think you could have heard him screaming, 'Noooooo!' four miles away!"

Everyone laughed for a few seconds and then Windmere spoke up: "We will be having a memorial service in honor of all those who gave their lives during this war tomorrow morning before noon. Everyone is invited to be there."

"I wouldn't miss it," Belinda replied.

"Neither would I," Victoria said.

"Good," Groman's voice came from behind the group. They all turned to see him slowly walking out of the healing tent towards them. "I had hoped you would stay long enough to attend."

Victoria nodded in agreement.

"Well, I will see you all tomorrow, then," Groman said. He turned to walk away but Victoria quickly rushed forward and hugged him.

"Thank you for protecting me," she whispered.

"It was what anyone, especially your brother, would have done," Groman replied quietly.

The two separated, and Victoria began to walk towards her own tent when she heard Windmere ask a question that made her freeze.

"Groman, I meant to ask you this yesterday, but I forgot. Where did you get that scar?"

Groman held up his hand and felt the two long scars that went across his face and over his right eye. "Oh, I...was cut by some out-of-control blades during a previous fight."

Windmere raised an eyebrow but didn't ask anything else. She and the rest of the group walked away aside from Hannela who walked silently alongside Victoria back to their shared tent where both were sound asleep within minutes.

That next morning, Victoria slept in until she was awoken to breakfast in her hammock that consisted of fried fish and eggs that had been caught and cooked by Hannela and Ripper. After eating the hearty meal, she soon found Jack and Dani waiting outside her tent. Dani excitedly held out her hand to show off the ring Trinia had made for her.

"Look at the ring! Isn't it incredible?" Dani asked.

Victoria looked at the golden ring with a round gemstone that seemed to be a swirl of ever-changing colors.

"It's very pretty, though you'll have to be careful wearing that around at home. No gemstone on earth changes colors like that," Victoria said.

"That's why I got this!" Dani said as she pulled out another ring. This one had a large fiery red diamond-like gemstone set into the top. "Trinia noticed me eyeing this one and let me have it too!"

"But as nice as those rings are, Dani and I are here to say goodbye," Jack said with a sad sigh.

"What?" Victoria said. "You're not staying for the service?"

Dani's face fell and she pointed to a swirling golden portal hidden behind Victoria's tent. "I don't know how to describe it, but we both feel we need to return home," she replied.

"Oh...okay," Victoria said as she quickly gave her friends a hug, which they readily returned.

"See you back on Earth?" Jack asked.

"Um...for your wedding? Absolutely!" Victoria replied.

"See you then!" Dani said as they walked into the portal and vanished from sight.

Victoria sighed and then heard some horns playing in the distance. It was a somber tune that got everyone's attention, and they all started making their way towards a large open clearing with a small hill in the middle of it that had a very large tree on its top.

Victoria made her way towards the crowd but saw Groman on the top of the hill with Annie and both of them were gesturing for her to go up there as well, which she reluctantly did.

When she got there, she was surprised to see that Groman had trimmed his beard and hair and had left The Empty Sword behind as well as his armor in favor of beautifully embroidered blue robes. Annie was wearing a gold dress and her fancy silver prosthetic legs as well. She quickly ran up to hug Victoria before stepping back and letting Groman speak.

"Would you like to say a few words today?" Groman asked quietly.

"I...I don't even know what I would say," Victoria replied. She looked out over the vast crowds of Kittrian, Trodontian, Amronian, Blackmian, Horiton, Flitnao, Fire Giant, Ice Dwarf, Unkarian, and Ibexian people.

"That is fine. You do not have to say anything," Groman said. He raised his hands, and the crowds quieted down. "People of Lulandal!" he shouted. "Today is the first morning of a new age for Lulandal: an age where we do not have to worry about some new enemy taking over our homes and hurting or killing our friends and family. Today is the start of something better! A bright dawn after a dark and stormy night.

"However, that dawn has come with a price that many of our own brave soldiers have paid; soldiers whose remains will be buried here with as much honor we can bestow regardless of what tribe they came from. They are all heroes to this world, and we will remember them as such; even those who did not come from this world but traveled from other worlds to aid us in our struggles against The Shadowed One and Falron. Stephen and all the other heroes who gave their lives in the hopes that we would be able to experience this new day did so willingly to ensure that no one else had to die.

"I am sure some of you are wondering, 'So now that Falron is gone, what do we do?'

"The answer is simple: We rebuild our homes; our towns; our cities and make them better than what they were before. And to that end, I would humbly request that all be made welcome here in Areiop. It would not matter what tribe they belong to, where they are from, or even if they are from this world. We are stronger together than when we are apart, and if we focus on uniting our peoples together, we can make Lulandal into a world that those who died would be proud of."

At that the people began cheering until Groman held up his hands for silence again before continuing.

"While we may certainly celebrate this victory, I would request that at least for today, we continue on in silence, to remember those who are not able to celebrate with us, whose voices we will not hear again, whose company we will be unable to cherish, and whose sacrifice we will never forget."

Groman stepped back and looked at Victoria. While she saw his smile, she could see his tears, too, as well as her own and Annie's.

The whole crowd stood in silence with nothing but the sound of the breeze going through the autumn leaves for several minutes until a singing voice broke the quiet air:

"Rest now my warrior, the battle is now over.

Thou hast fought well and now greatly honored.

The sun rises, the battlefield, its light does now cover,

Your allies assembled; their admiration garnered.

Sleep now in the peace that silence brings

And rise to the lands above on golden wings."

It was Annie, singing that song she and Groman had been talking about that first morning back in Lulandal. Victoria listened as Annie continued singing as she was joined by many others in the crowd. Soon, the whole glade was filled with the tune as even those who didn't know the words were joining in by humming along.

Victoria scanned the crowd, and she could see there wasn't a dry eye among them.

*You did it, Steve,* she thought. *It is all thanks to you and The One Above.*

The rest of the day was filled with a large-yet-somber feast in honor of the victory. Victoria found herself seated at the table of honor once again with some of the other heroes from that battle. She ate her fill and then she walked for a little while to the western ridge where they had charged into battle a day prior. There, in the shadow of some trees, she sat in the grass and watched as the rebuilding efforts were beginning in the ruined city.

Time seemed to move quickly, as the next thing Victoria knew, the sun was beginning to set behind her. She remembered a familiar feeling, and she pulled out the photo of her and her family at the park from her pocket and could see the similarities between that sunset and the one she was witnessing right now.

"Hey, sweetheart," Belinda's voice said quietly behind her. "I just finished talking with Vesuvian. Are you ready to go home?"

"What did he say?" Victoria asked without turning around.

"He just wants the armor to remain here and, if possible, made into a memorial to all those who lost their lives in the Blackmian war. I've already agreed to those terms," Belinda said calmly.

Victoria stood up and turned to face her great aunt, the photo still in her hand.

Belinda walked over to Victoria and gently took the photo from her and looked at it. "I remember your mother complaining about this trip," Belinda said with a chuckle. "Yes, she said the rain, the bugs, and the heat were murder. But she still said she enjoyed being on that trip as she was with all of you. Being with you meant everything to her. But I know you understand that all too well."

Belinda handed the photo back to Victoria who looked at it again and then looked back at Areiop, only to see Groman and Annie standing a little way off, their clothes gently blowing in the breeze.

"You'd better say your goodbyes before we go," Belinda said as she turned to walk back towards the gateway to Earth.

"Great Aunt Belinda…" Victoria said hesitantly, "…I'm not sure I want to go back to Earth just yet."

Belinda turned around with a confused expression on her face. "What do you mean, Tori?" she asked quietly.

"It's just that…other than you, there's nothing really left for me there…" Victoria replied. "I have friends on Earth, yes, but I have some friends here, too, whom I'm not sure I want to say goodbye to."

A look of understanding came over Belinda's face as she quickly hugged Victoria tightly. "I know what you mean, my dear," she said quietly through her tears. "Just be sure to stop by and say hello from time to time. It's going to be awful lonely at the farm without you and Stephen around."

"I will. I promise," Victoria said as her own eyes were welling up.

Belinda grabbed her shoulders and looked Victoria in the eyes. "You've always been like the daughter I've never had. I wish you the best in your life here," Belinda said quietly before hugging Victoria again.

"Thank you, Auntie," Victoria replied quietly.

The two separated from their embrace, and Victoria turned back and walked towards her two friends who were waiting for her.

"We just came to say good-" Annie began before Victoria cut her off with a hug.

"No, no goodbyes, not this time," Victoria said.

"Wait, you... you mean...?!" Groman said in surprise.

"I'd like to take you up on your offer of everyone being welcome to live in Areiop," Victoria said. "Do you think I would be welcome here?"

"Of course!" Groman said quickly before catching himself and clearing his throat. "I mean, of course, you would be welcome here; you are a hero to the people, after all. I know they would be thrilled to have you live among us."

"Come on! Let us go pick out a house for you!" Annie said excitedly as she started pulling Victoria by her left hand. Victoria held out her right hand to Groman, who hesitantly took it, and together, the three of them walked down the ridge towards the city.

Back up on the hill, Belinda watched them go with tears in her eyes but a smile on her face.

*Jillian*, she thought to herself. *My sweet niece. I hope you are as happy about your little girl growing up as I am.*

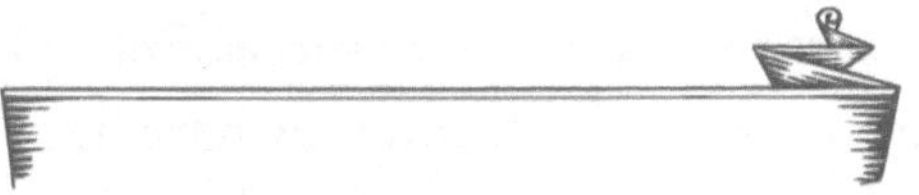

# Chapter 14. New Beginnings, New Life. (Ten years later)

Groman steadily walked through the fall foliage, listening to the leaves crunch under his worn leather boots. He looked around at the cemetery he was traveling through until he spotted what he had been searching for: a small clearing in the woods off to the side of the cemetery. He quickened his pace and was there within minutes.

"Sorry it took me so long to find you again," he said with a chuckle. "I know I have not visited you in a while, but all my responsibilities as an elder have been increased recently."

He looked over the large headstone made from a grey rock that had been polished until it shone in the evening light. He glanced at his reflection in the stone. *I should probably trim my beard again*, he mused as he looked at the white hair that went well past his chin. He glanced at the sword that had been inserted into the top of the headstone. The Servant's Sword looked like it was fresh from the forge, even though it had been set in the stone for the last ten years.

Groman then sat down in front of the headstone and read the inscription: "Stephen Higdon. Not from this world but gave his life for it so that we might be free from evil." He sighed. "Some days, I cannot believe it has been ten years now, since we lost you in the fight against Falron," he then spoke in the direction of the grave, "and a lot has happened in those ten years. We have successfully rebuilt all the cities that were lost to Falron's control, and they have been steadily growing in the years since. We built a series of roadways to connect all of the cities and towns, and resulting trade has helped everyone to prosper as new businesses start up where there had not been any before.

"Trakken and Trinia moved to Areiop shortly after their marriage, they now run the best jewelry shop and smithy in town, and have three beautiful children as well. As I may have mentioned before, your sister opened up her own Tavern and Inn a year after our victory; it has steadily grown to be one of the local landmarks, and now, everyone knows of The Warrior's Rest. Saralia has a traveling fur business, though she likes to split most of her time between here and Prarait, where her mother has retired from a life of fighting to work at her smithy at her leisure. As for our other friends, Monaria has stayed on as an ambassador of the Flitnao people and advisor to me. Tiny has taken up a position as the commander of the Black Peak Prison and has been doing a wondrous job in rehabilitating the other Unkarians and helping them return to a life out from beneath the mountain to the sunlight once more. Annie is now a full-time healer, just as I had wanted to be. She and the old healer Henton keep everyone in good shape. And as for me...well, today, I was offered to become the king of the Kittrian again. It seems they will not let that idea go. I declined it again, but when they offered me the title of 'Lord Protector of the Kittrian people,' I accepted after getting some advice from my wife."

Just then, Groman heard the sounds of multiple people walking through the leaves towards him. He quickly stood up and looked around. Hearing the sounds of childish laughter, he calmed down and soon spotted the source.

Four children were making their way towards him: two boys and two girls. The eldest boy in front had short black hair, pointed ears, and green cat-like eyes, but five fingers gripped a walking stick he held in his right hand. He was wearing a brown tunic and trousers with a small dagger on the belt as well as a green cloak.

"Hello, Father!" the boy called out.

"Hello, Son," Groman replied with a smile. "Did you all come looking for me?"

"Yes, sir," the younger boy replied. He looked like his brother but had short white hair and yellow eyes. He had a blue shirt and black trousers. A small bow and quiver of arrows were on his back.

"Well, Aldric, I did tell you that I was going to be here until dinner was ready," Groman said.

"And we are here to tell you that dinner is ready!" the youngest daughter replied. She bounced up and down with excitement, her long white hair getting all messed up and her orange eyes glowing with happiness. She was wearing a rose red dress with a white apron with a blue cloak.

"Thank you, Bree," Groman said with a warm smile before turning to his eldest daughter, who was wearing a long green dress with a green cloak to match. Two daggers hung on her belt, one on each side. "Hope, you are among only family here, do you really feel you need to wear that?" he asked quietly.

Hope anxiously tugged at a lock of her silver hair and looked at her father, her blue right eye looking on as she felt his gaze on the patch over her left eye. "Well..." she began.

"No one is going to tease you here," Groman said gently as he took a knee in front of her. He gently removed the eye patch to reveal her left eye, which was a brilliant bright yellow.

"I just wish I didn't look like this," Hope said quietly.

"Now, Hope, what have your mother and I said to you almost a hundred times now?" Groman asked quietly.

"That The One Above made me who I am, and he never makes mistakes. Everyone and everything has a purpose," Hope said sheepishly.

"That is correct!" Groman said. "He has a plan for you and made you perfect just the way you are."

Hope sighed quietly while looking at the ground. "Can I have my patch back, now?"

"Of course, my dear. Could you maybe leave it off for now until we go back to town?" Groman asked as he handed the patch back to his daughter before standing up and looking around at his children. "Now, where is your mother? I do hope she did not let you wander out here by yourselves."

"I'm right behind you, my love."

Victoria's voice came from behind Groman's back. He jumped and spun around, much to the amusement of their children. There, he saw her, wearing the long emerald green dress she loved so much, her long black hair blowing in the gentle breeze, and their fifth child, a little boy, in her arms fast asleep.

"You completed your mission with honor, my dears," Victoria said with a laugh.

"Oh? What might that mission have been, my dear Lady Victoria?" Groman asked playfully.

"We were to distract you, so Mom could scare you again," the eldest son replied.

"Well, Stephen, you did your job well. I say we all should go back home and enjoy the wonderful meal your Aunt Annie has prepared for us," Groman said with a laugh.

"Honey, before you go, I wanted to tell you Monaria came looking for you back at the house. She was saying something about silence coming to our world?"

"That sounds odd. Do you think she meant it as peace and quiet?" Groman asked.

"I don't know. But I'd like to have a few minutes alone here, if you don't mind," Victoria said quietly.

"Of course, my love," Groman said as he gently took the sleeping toddler from Victoria's arms. "Come along, now, children. Your mother wants to let you have first pick of the desserts before you eat your dinner!"

The children all cheered, and Victoria quietly laughed before giving Groman a mock glare.

"Oh, no!" Groman said in a mock scared tone. "Your mother is giving me the look, we best hurry home before she catches us!"

Groman and the children all laughed as they raced away towards the city, leaving Victoria alone at her brother's grave site.

After a few minutes of facing the headstone in silence, Victoria finally spoke: "Hey, Steve. I know I know it's been a while. Being a mother to five energetic kids keeps me really busy, and I haven't had as much time to visit as I wanted to." She sat down in the soft grass and looked at the many flowers that had been planted around the glade. "Annie was right...those flowers really help light up the area." She looked at the inscription on the headstone again, and tears began to well up in her eyes. "I wanted to say I'm sorry. I'm sorry for being so angry at you the day you left us. I was angry because you took yourself away from me when I thought I needed you most. In my mind, I called you selfish and dumb for letting yourself die like that. But now that I'm a mother...I think I know what you were thinking that day. My children may be learning how to defend themselves, especially Stephen Jr., Aldric, and Hope, but I know they may face an opponent whom they can't defeat on their own. If the time were to come that they were in danger...I would throw myself in front of the killing blow in a heartbeat. My love for them is also a desire to protect them...and I think that's what you felt too. So, I am sorry for what I may have said or even thought those ten years ago."

Victoria sat in silence, listening to the wind in the trees and the birds singing around her. Their tune seemed to stir something in Victoria, and she stood up and recalled something she had heard those ten years ago during the memorial service. She began to sing....

*Rest now my warrior, the battle is now over.*
*Thou hast fought well and now greatly honored.*
*The sun rises, the battlefield, its light does now cover,*
*Your allies assembled; their admiration garnered.*
*Sleep now in the peace that silence brings*
*And rise to the lands above on golden wings.*
*Rest now my friend, our hardship is ended.*
*Through the struggle we stayed side by side.*
*Though broken at times, our friendship always mended,*
*Our bond strong as metal and like a rope tied.*
*Sleep now in the knowledge I am safe*
*And that we will meet again because of our faith.*
*Rest now my hero, the world is at peace.*
*The enemy is gone, the people secure.*
*The prisoners returned, hope increased.*
*The homes rebuilt, and life ensure.*
*Sleep now, for your mission is at an end*
*And to the lands above, you may now ascend.*

After she finished singing, she looked back at the headstone. She felt more at peace now and decided to turn back towards her home. But before she walked out of the glade, she looked back at the stone one more time. She saw the setting sun reflect off The Servant's Sword with a dazzling brilliance of red and yellow before the light disappeared completely.

"I'll see you again someday brother," Victoria said quietly. "Until then, keep watching my back, will you?"

With that, Lady Victoria of Areiop walked back through the cemetery and returned home to her family and friends.

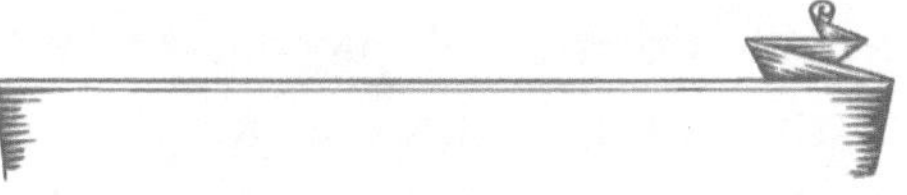

# Chapter 15 Epilogue.
# (Present Day)

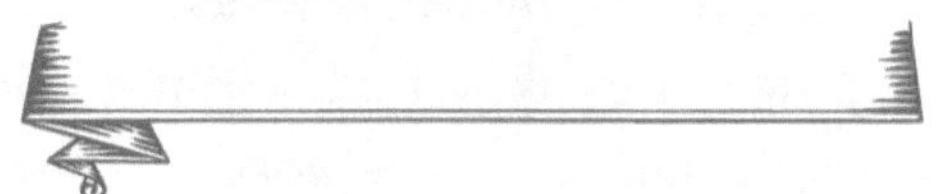

A young man sat in a chair in his tiny apartment, looking at the cursor blink on his laptop. He wanted to write something, but his mind just wasn't working today.

"What do you think, Rufus?" he said, looking at his tuxedo cat who was lazily wandering into the room. "Do you think I should try and make up a story about those people who appeared downstairs two days ago?"

The cat just yawned and went into his litter box.

"Yeah," the man said with a laugh. "Nobody would believe me, even if I wasn't making the whole thing up."

He got up from his chair and grabbed a jacket from its place on a wooden chair.

"Maybe some fresh air will help inspire me," he said. He reached for the doorknob to leave but a sudden noise made him stop.

*Thunk.*

Something large had hit the window. The man and his cat both looked at the window to see something large was clinging to the window screen.

"What on earth?" the man asked as he slid the window open. As he did whatever it was flew away. He removed the screen and poked his head out and looked around at the city outside.

"Must have been another dumb pigeon," he said, looking back at the cat who was staring at him with wide eyes.

Suddenly, a flash of red burst through the window and into the apartment. The cat puffed up his tail and rocketed under the bed in the adjoining room. The man looked at what came in: It was a large red lizard, a little bigger than the size of a cat, with six legs, a tail that split in two, and large fleshy wings which it used to fly around. It was making chirping noises like a bird, and it finally landed on the windowsill displaying its tail. The man looked in surprise as he saw a piece of paper tied to it with a piece of string. He gently untied the string and looked at the paper.

*To my friend, The Author,*

*I regret to inform you that my brother will be unable to return the weapon you gave him. Sadly, he perished in the battles against Falron the Feared, and the weapon was lost. I wish I could have returned it to you, as you had been a help towards us. But I can only send you this letter of apology. The people of Lulandal send their thanks for your gift and wish they could repay you somehow. You need only send a reply with Little Flyer.*

*With regards,*

*Victoria of Lulandal and Groman of The Empty Sword.*

The man looked at the paper in shock. It was real! It was all real! He heard a scrabbling sound coming from the window and saw the lizard was making its way outside.

"Wait!" he said as he frantically looked for a usable pen and paper. "Can you take a message back with you?"

He felt stupid for even asking an animal a question, but to his surprise, the lizard looked back at him as if to say, "Duh, of course I can."

Finding a pen and piece of note paper, the man quickly wrote:

*To Victoria,*

*I just wanted to say you have my deepest sympathy for the loss of your brother. Do not worry about that old shotgun. I only hope your brother found it useful in his final battle.*

*If I may be so bold, as I am an aspiring writer and am looking for some story ideas to turn into books, could you by chance tell me more of your adventures in that other world? I think they have some potential to be an incredible series.*

*With best wishes,*

*The Author.*

The Author rolled up the note and tied it to the lizards awaiting tail. No sooner was the knot tied than the lizard quickly took off into the afternoon sun. The Author quietly replaced the window screen and looked down to see his cat emerge from under the bed, his tail still puffed and back arched.

"Scaredy cat," The Author said jokingly before sitting down at his laptop and looking at the screen again. He began to type on his keyboard and stopped when he finished the title.

*The Empty Sword Saga. Book 1.*

He leaned back in the chair and looked at the title again.

"This is gonna be great!" he said with a smile.

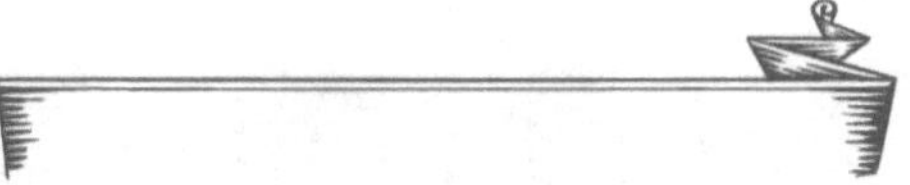

# The Hero's Hymn

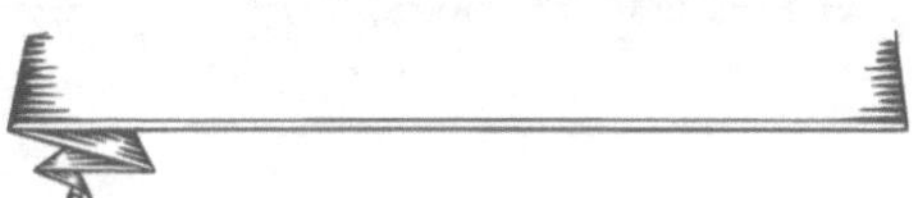

*Traditional Lulandal Melody Lyrics Adapted by Jonathan Zobel*
*Adapted by Kayle Buchanan*

♩ = 92

1.Rest my warr - ior, the batt - le is now o - ver;
2.Rest my friend, _ our hard-ship is now end - ed;
3.Rest my he - ro, the world is now at peace; _

Thou hast fought well, and
Through the strug - gle, we
Dan - ger all gone, the

now are great-ly hon - ored. _
stay-ed side by side. _
peo-ple now se - cur - ed. _

The sun ri - ses, its rays cast o'er the batt - le field;
Of - ten splin-tered, our friend-ship al-ways mend - ed;
Capt-tives re-turned, brought back to love and laugh - ter;

Friends a - ssem-bled, their ad - mir - a - tion gar - nered.
Our bond now strong as three strands sure - ly tied. _
The homes re - built, a life of hope en - sur - ed.

Sleep now, in the
Sleep now, and _
Sleep now, for your

peace that si-lence brings; _ Rise to the land a-bove on _ go - ld - en wings.
know that I am safe, _ And we will meet a-gain be - cause of our faith.
miss-ion's at its end, _ And to the land a-bove you _ may now a - scend.

1, 2.

3.

# About the Author

Hi there! I'm Jonathan Zobel, the author of this book. I'm a big history nut and I grew up reading many many books throughout my childhood and teen years and I've always enjoyed a good story. I was homeschooled by my parent's all the way through high shcool and I attended Faith Baptist Bible college in Ankeny IA for two years, graduating with an AA. I was a playwright for a few years before I shifted to writing books.

www.ingramcontent.com/pod-product-compliance
Lightning Source LLC
Chambersburg PA
CBHW021959120726
47992CB00001B/325